TERROR IN ARKHAM

When Ambrose Dewart returned to the ancient family estate in the brooding hills of northern Massachusetts, its isolation powerfully impressed him. And being of a reclusive nature, he immediately set about rehabilitating the old place as his permanent home.

But an old document, handed down from a great grandfather of sinister reputation, laid down certain injunctions . . . injunctions that were never to be flouted:

Never invite HIM that lurks at the threshold!

That was the most important injunction of all.

But Dewart had an inquisitive nature, and he wanted to see what would happen if . . .

THE LURKER
AT THE
THRESHOLD

H. P. Lovecraft
and
August Derleth

BALLANTINE BOOKS • NEW YORK

ISBN 0-345-25077-X-150

The edition published by arrangement with Arkham House.

Manufactured in the United States of America

First Ballantine Books Edition: March, 1971
Third Printing: April, 1976

1

Billington's Wood

NORTH OF ARKHAM THE HILLS RISE DARK, WILD, AND wooded, and much overgrown, an area through which the Miskatonic flows seaward, almost at one boundary of the wooded tract. Travellers in this region are seldom impelled to go beyond the outskirts of the wood, though a faint track leads into it and presumably goes through the hills, and beyond the hills, to the Miskatonic, and beyond that into open country once more. What deserted houses have been left by the ravages of time bear a surprisingly uniform aspect of weather-beaten squalor, and, while the wooded region itself shows signs of singular vitality, there seems to be little evidence of fertility in the country around. Indeed, a traveller on the Aylesbury Pike, which opens from River Street in Arkham, and proceeds in leisurely fashion west and northwest of the ancient, gambrel-roofed town towards the strange, lonely Dunwich country beyond Dean's Corners, cannot help but be impressed with the remarkable degree of what, at first glance, might seem reforestation in that region, but which, on closer examination, proves to be not new growth, but ancient, hardy trees flourishing, it seems, centuries after time should have taken its toll of them.

Arkham people have forgotten almost all about it; there were legends, dark and vague, which their grand-dames brooded about at the fireside, some of them harkening back to the time of the witchcraft fever; but like so many similar tales, their tenuousness eventually slipped completely away, and nothing was left to be said but that the wood was 'Billington's Wood,' and the hills were 'Mr. Billington's,' and all that property around, including the great house which could not be seen but was none the less there, deep in that wood, on a pleasant knoll, it was said, 'near the tower and the circle of stones.' The gnarled, old trees invited none of the curious, the dark wood beckoned no traveller, not even the horde of scavengers in search of antiquities of customs, legends, and household appurtenances, who might conceivably have been drawn to the old Billington house. The wood was shunned; the casual traveller hastened by, urged on by a curious dislike for which he had no explanation, by his fancies and his imagination, which left him no regrets and brought him safely home again, whether he came from Arkham or Boston or from the lost hamlets of the Massachusetts countryside.

'Old Billington' was remembered, drawn from the memory of ancients long dead in Arkham. Alijah Billington had been his name, and his station that of a country squire in the early nineteenth century. He had come to live in that house which had been his grandfather's and his great-grandfather's before him; and in his old age he had departed for his ancestral shores, the country south of London, in England. Thenceforth nothing was heard of him, though the taxes were duly paid by a firm of solicitors, whose address in Middle Temple lent dignity to the legend of Old Billington. The decades duly passed; presumably Alijah Billington was gathered to his ancestors, and his solicitors likewise; equally certain was it that Alijah's son Laban reached his majority and the sons of his father's solicitors repeated the natural pattern; for, though the decades passed, the required fees to satisfy the annual tax-assessment made against the deserted property were duly deposited through a New York bank, and the property continued to bear the name of Billington, though, somewhere about the turn of the twentieth century, there was to be heard a tale that the last of the Billington men, who would have been Laban's son, no doubt, had left no male issue, and the line had been continued by his daughter, whose name was not known, save as a 'Mrs. Dewart,' but this casual of gossip was of no interest to the natives of Arkham and was soon forgotten, for what was a Mrs. Dewart whom they had never seen to them against the receding memory of Old Billington and his 'noises'?

This was the thing remembered of Old Billington, and it was especially remembered by the descendants of a few old armigerous families who made a practice of accounting for the local gentry through the generations, if possible. But so effective had been the inroads of time that no specific story survived; it was said only that noises had been heard often at dusk and in the night among the wooded hills where Billington lived, but it was not clear whether Ailjah himself was responsible for them, or whether they had some other source. In plain fact, Alijah Billington would have been totally forgotten if it had not been for the forbidden wood and the wilderness of that lush growth, and for the hidden marshland deep in the heart of the wood near the house, from which arose in the spring nights such a piping and croaking of frogs as was heard nowhere else within a radius of a hundred miles of Arkham, and from which in the summer came an almost unnatural glow which flickered and danced on the low-hung clouds on nights of louring weather, coming, it was generally agreed, from the hordes of fireflies which had occupied that place, together with the frogs, and sundry other creatures and insects for unbroken time. The noises had ceased with Alijah Billington's departure, but the piping of the frogs continued, and the glowing of the fireflies was not diminished, nor, of summer nights, was the chorus of the whippoorwills lessened to any degree.

After so many years of desertion, the news that the great old house would be opened, which came out one day in March, 1921, was a mattter of increasing curiosity and interest to the dwellers of the country around. There appeared in the columns of the Arkham *Advertiser* a brief and succinct notice stating that Mr. Am-

4

brose Dewart desired assistance in repairing and refurbishing the 'Billington House,' and that application might be made to him in person at his room in the Hotel Miskatonic, which was actually a kind of dormitory used in connection with and on the grounds of Miskatonic University, overlooking the Quadrangle. Mr. Ambrose Dewart turned out to be a hawk-faced man of medium height, chiefly distinguished for a flare of red hair which gave him a tonsured appearance, keen of eye and tight of lip, exceedingly correct and possessed of a dry sort of humour which made a favourable impression on those labouring men whom he hired.

Before another day dawned, it was known in Arkham that Ambrose Dewart was indeed the lineal descendant of Alijah Billington; that he had made a pilgrimage to the shores of the country his ancestors had adopted as their own for three generations or more, and now meant to return. He was a man of some fifty years of age, brown-skinned, who had lost his only son in the great war, and, having no other issue, he had turned towards America as the haven in which he desired to spend the rest of his days. He had come into Massachusetts a fortnight ago to examine his property; what he had found there evidently satisfied him, for he had made plans to restore the old house to all its former glory, though he soon learned that for the time being he would need to abate his desire for certain aspects of modernity he had sought, such as electricity, for the nearest line ran several miles away, and there were mechanical difficulties to be overcome before electricity could be installed. But, for the rest of his plans, there was no reason to delay, and all that spring the work went forward, the house was restored, a road was put through to it, and beyond it to the far side of the wood, and in the summer, Mr. Ambrose Dewart formally took possession, abandoning his lodgings in Arkham, and his labouringmen were dismissed with a handsome bonus, to return to their native places filled with awe and wonder about the appointments of Old

Billington's house and its resemblance to the Craigie House of Cambridge, long occupied by the poet, Longfellow, about the fine old staircase with its impressive carvings, and the study that was fully two storeys in height and had in one wall a great window of many-coloured glass, which looked out upon the west, about the library, which had been untouched by human hands for all those years, and about the various appurtenances which Mr. Dewart had pronounced of great value for anyone who took his simple pleasure in old things.

Soon there was talk of this and of that, and presently there was a conscious excavation for specific memories of Old Billington, who, it was said, was not unlike his descendant in appearance. In the course of the speculation which grew, there came from the country around Dunwich once more the tale of the 'noises' which Old Billington had brought about, and sundry other tales of somewhat sinister complexion began to be whispered about, though none could point to their source, save only that they had come from that portion of the Dunwich country where the Whateleys and the Bishops and a last few of the armigerous families lived in various degrees of decay and dissolution. Because the Whateleys and the Bishops, too, had lived in that region of Massachusetts for many generations, and were indeed contemporaneous in their ancestry with not only Old Billington but with the very first Billington—he who had built that great house with the 'rose window,' as they called it, though it was not that; and it was presumed that the tales they told had come down through the generations gone by, and were at least akin to truth if not exactly factual, so that there was immediately a revival of interest in Billington's Wood and in Mr. Dewart himself.

Ambrose Dewart, however, was happily unaware of the speculation and gossip his strange coming had aroused. He was of a solitary nature, and revelled in the solitude in which he now found himself; his primary determination was to inform himself as completely as possible of the advantages of his property, and to that end he bent himself assiduously, though, if the truth must be told, he hardly knew where to begin. His mother had told him nothing at all about his property, save that the family owned 'some property' in the 'Commonwealth of Massachusetts,' which it would be 'wise' not to sell, but to keep in the family always, even to the extent that if something should happen to him and/or to his son, it should go to his Boston cousin, Stephen Bates, whom he had never seen. Indeed, there had been left for him only a puzzling set of instructions, which had evidently come down to him from that Alijah Billington who had left his property behind him when he set forth for England, a series of directives for which Ambrose Dewart could not account at all, quite possibly because he was not yet familiar enough with his property to do so.

He was adjured, for instance, 'not to cause the water to cease flowing about the island,' nor to 'molest the tower,' nor to 'entreat of the stones,' nor to 'open the door which leads to strange time and place,' nor yet to 'touch upon the window seeking to change it.' These instructions meant nothing to Dewart, though they fascinated him, and, once having read them, he could not get them out of his mind, they kept returning to him and running through his thoughts like a rune, and thus insidiously goaded him to poke and putter about through the house and the wood, among the hills and the marshland area, so that in time he discovered that the house was not the only building on the property he owned, but that it held also a very old stone tower, which rose upon what seemed at one time to have been a little island in the midst of a stream which had once rushed down from the hills as a tributary to the Miskatonic, but which had long since gone dry in all but the spring months.

He discovered this late one afternoon in August, and was immediately convinced that it was to this tower that his ancestor's instructions related. Therefore he examined it with close attention, and found it to be a cylindrical tower of stone with a conical roof, the whole being perhaps twelve feet in diameter and some twenty feet high. There had apparently been at one time a great arched opening, which suggested that the tower had originally been roofless, but this had been sealed up with masonry. Dewart, who was not ill-informed on architectural matters, was much taken up with this structure, for it required no skilled eye to ascertain that its stones were indeed very ancient, more so, it seemed, than the house itself. He had with him a small magnifying glass with which he had been studying certain very old Latin texts in the library of the house, and with this he scrutinized the stone masonry and discovered that it was dressed, and showed an odd and unknown technique, which involved the use of what appeared to be geometrical designs similar to those which had been scratched in larger drawings upon the stones which had been utilized to seal up the archway. Of singular fascination, also, was the tower's base, which was of remarkable thickness, and gave the appearance of being fixed in the earth at a great depth; but this, Dewart reasoned, might very possibly be because the ground level had risen in the interval since last Alijah Billington had looked upon it.

Had Alijah then built it? It seemed, at least in part, of greater age, and since this was so, by whose hands had it been erected? The problem intrigued Dewart, and, since he had already been made aware of many old papers among the volumes of his ancestor's library, he dared to hope that some reference to the tower would be found therein, and to the end of examining them, he finally turned back towards the house, though not, however, before he had stood off at a little distance and scrutinized the tower, seeing then for the first time that it rose in what must at one time have been a circle of stones, which to his delight he identified as similar in many ways to the Druidic remains at Stonehenge. Water had clearly once flowed on both sides of the

8

little island, and evidently in some quantity, for the marks of erosion were not yet worn away, despite the encroachment of the thick undergrowth, and the inevitable excoriation of countless rains and winds which found no barrier to keep them away, as had the somewhat superstitious natives.

Dewart made haste slowly. It was dusk when he arrived back at the house, owing in large part to the necessity of skirting the marshy area, which lay between the site of the tower and the knoll upon which the house stood. He prepared himself a repast, and while he ate it, he considered how best he might embark upon that investigation upon which he had now fixed his course. The papers left in the study were for the most part very old; it would be impossible to read some of them, for they would crumble to nothing. Fortunately, however, some scattered sheets were of parchment, and thus possible to handle without fear of destruction, and there was also a small leather-bound book inscribed in a childish hand, 'Laban B.,' which must presumably be the son of the Alijah who had departed this land for England more than a century ago. After due thought, Dewart determined to begin with the child's daybook, for such it proved to be.

He read by lamplight, the problem of electricity having been engulfed in a morass of officialdom in some remote corner of the Commonwealth, from which it was promised that a workable solution would eventually emerge. The lamplight, together with the yellow glowing from the hearth—for he had lit a fire there, the night being somewhat cool—gave the study a comfortable feeling of intimacy, and Dewart was soon lost in the past as it rose out of the scrawl on the yellowed pages before him. The child, Laban, who was, Dewart determined, his own great-grandfather, was evidently precocious, for his age at the beginning of the book was given as nine, and at the end, as Dewart ascertained by turning there, as eleven; and he had clearly a good eye

9

for detail, in so far that his chroniclings were not solely devoted to the happenings of the household.

It was soon manifest that the boy was motherless, and that his only companion appeared to be an Indian, a Narragansett, who was in Alijah Billington's service. His name was given alternately as Quamus or Quamis, the boy apparently not being certain which it was, and he was evidently closer to Alijah's age than to the boy's, for the attitude of respect which was manifest in Laban's large-lettered chroniclings was out of proportion to what it would have been if his companion were of his own age. The daybook began with a recital of the boy's routine, but, once having set his routine down, the boy did not afterwards refer to it except as something accomplished. Instead, he devoted his writings to accounts of what had been done by him in the few hours of afternoon during which he was free of his studies, and might roam as he pleased in the house, or, provided that he was companioned by the Indian, in the woods, though he set down that he had been discouraged from wandering far from the house.

The Indian was obviously either very silent and uncommunicative, or he was loquacious in repeating to the boy some of the legends of his tribe; the boy, being imaginative, took pleasure in his company no matter what the Indian's mood, and occasionally put down in his daybook something of the narratives told him by his companion, who, it became plain from the account as it progressed, also did some kind of work for Alijah, 'after the hour at which the supper is served.'

Along about the middle of the daybook, an hiatus occurred; several pages had been torn out and not replaced, so that there was a period for which there was no accounting in Laban's handwriting. Immediately thereafter occurred an entry under date of March seventeenth (the year not given), which Dewart read with mounting interest and speculation, since the absence of the preceding pages emphasized the suggestiveness of the account.

'Today, following the hour of last study, we went out into the snowfall, and Quamis went around the marsh, leaving me to wait for him on a fallen bole, which I did not much like, and as a result I concluded it would be as good if not better to follow him; so I set forth upon the trail he left in the new-fallen snow, which descended last night, and presently came upon him once more where Father has forbidden us to go, on the banks of the stream across from that place where the tower rises. He was on his knees and had his arms raised up, and he was saying in a loud voice words in his own language which I could not understand, having been taught too little of it, but that had the sound of *Narlato*, or *Narlotep*. I was about to call out to him, when he saw me, and, immediately getting up to his feet, he came to where I was and took me by the hand and led me away from that place; whereupon I inquired of him whether he prayed, or what he had done, and why he did not pray in that chapel built by the men of the white race who were missionaries among his people; but he did not answer, save only to say to me that I must not tell my father where we had been, lest he, Quamis, be punished for having gone to that place against the orders of his employer. But the place being barren among the rocks and inaccessible for the waters around it, holds for me no attraction, whatever it is that Quamis finds to draw him thither against my father's wishes.'

Then for two days there were but commonplace entries, after which followed a guarded sentence which indicated that Alijah had discovered the Indian's defection, and had punished him, but how, the boy had not chronicled. After seven further entries, there was another reference to the 'forbidden place'; this time the boy and the Indian had been caught in a sudden snowstorm, and had lost their way. They stumbled about this way and that, the snow being very thick, and falling upon soft ground, which had opened to the late March sun, with the snow being blown into their eyes,

11

and presently 'we were come upon a place strange to, me, but Quamis gave a great cry and strove to hustle me away, and I saw that we had come to the brook which flowed about the isle of stones and the tower, but this time we had approached it from the far side. How we had come thither I did not know, for we had set out in the opposite direction, to the east, intending to walk over toward the Miskatonic River, unless it be that the snow so suddenly come upon us had confused us to so great a degree. The great haste and the seeming fear Quamis shewed, impelled me once again to inquire of him what caused him these qualms, but he only answered me as before, that my father "does not wish it"—which is to say, he does not want me in this area, though I have freedom to roam in whatever other parts of his land I choose, and may go even into Arkham, though I am forbidden to go in the direction of either Dunwich or Innsmouth, and must not past time in the Indian village which is in the hills past Dunwich.'

Thereafter there was no further reference to the tower, but instead there were certain other curious paragraphs. Three days after the entry concerning the sudden snowstorm, the boy recorded a quick thaw which 'rid the earth of snow.' And that night, as he recorded on the following morning, 'I was awak'd from my sleep by strange noises in the hills, as of great cries, and I started up and went first to the east window, and there did see nothing, and then to the south, and there likewise did see nothing; after which, summoning my courage, I crept from my room and crossed the hall and rapped on my father's door, but he made no answer and I thinking he had not heard me, dared to open the door and go into his room, where I walked straight to his bed, but was much disturbed to find him not in it, and no sign to shew that he had that night been in it; and, chancing to look from the west window of his room I was made aware of a kind of blue or green glow that shone above the trees in the Hollow of the hills lying over to the west, whereat I was much given to wonder, for it was from this direction that the sounds I had heard seemed to come and still came—as it were, great screams, but in no human voice or even in the voice of any beast known to me; and it seemed to me, as I stood there at the partly-open window transfixed by fear and wonder, that other voices similar to these came from far off in the direction of Dunwich or Innsmouth and lay in the air like great echoes high up in the sky. After a little while these came to an end, and the glowing in the heavens ended, too, and I went back to bed; but this morning, when Quamis came, I asked him what it was had made such a noise in the night; whereupon he answered me that I had been dreaming and did not know whereof I spoke, and should say nothing of it to *him,* and abide by my own counsel; so I did not tell him what I had seen, for he seemed in truth sore troubled at my words, as if he feared my father would hear me even as I spoke. I was of a mind to bespeak my anxiety concerning my father's safety, but by what Quamis said, I knew my father was in the house and like to be in his room, sleeping late, so I did not press this but made pretence of forgetting what I had heard and seen, even as Quamis said I must do, whereat Quamis felt easier in spirit and no longer seemed so distressed.'

For fully a fortnight thereafter Laban's entries concerned trivial matters, such as his studies and his reading. Then once more occurred a cryptic reference, brief and pointed. 'The noises do seem to come from the west with singular persistence, but there is surely a crying of answer from the east by northeast, which is the direction of Dunwich, or the wild country around Dunwich.' Again, four days thereafter, the boy wrote that he had scarcely been put to bed, when, having arisen to watch the setting of the new moon, he saw his father outside the house. 'He was accompanied by Quamis, and both carried something, but I could not make out what it was. In a short time they disappeared around the house, walking eastward, and I crossed to my father's room to look further for them, but saw them not, though I heard my father's voice rising in the wood.' Later that night, he had been awakened again by 'great noises, as before, and I lay listening to them, and determined that sometimes they arose in a kind of chant, and sometimes in flat, terrible screamings which were not good to hear.' There were similar entries for some time thereafter, and in this fashion almost a year was accounted for.

The next to final entry was extremely puzzling. All night long the boy had heard the 'great noises' in the hills, and it seemed to him that all the world must hear these voices rising in the brooding darkness, and in the morning, 'not seeing him, I inquired after Quamis, and was told that Quamis had "gone away" and would not be back, and that, moreover, we too were going ere nightfall, taking very little baggage with us, and I was told to make myself ready. My father appeared to be in a dreadful fret to be off, though he did not say whither we were going; but I assumed it to be Arkham, or perhaps, at most far, Boston or Concord, but I did not question, and quickened myself to obey, not knowing what to take with me, but trying to select such articles as I would most need for a visit, such as clean breeches and the like. I was much puzzled by my father's haste, and by his concern with the time; for he was very eager to leave the house not later than mid-afternoon, and said that he had "a deal to get done with" before we would go; none the less, he found time to inquire of me several times whether I was ready, whether I had finished my packing, &c.'

The final entry in the book, which was some pages from its end, had been made that afternoon. 'My father says we are going to England. We shall sail across the ocean and visit relatives in that country. It is now mid-afternoon and my father is almost ready.' To this he had added, with an almost defiant flourish of the pen:

14

'This is the daybook of Laban Billington, son of Alijah and Lavinia Billington, aet. 11 yrs. this day sennight.

Dewart closed the book in some perplexity, and yet with keen interest. Beyond the unseeing words the boy had put down there lay a major puzzle, of which, unfortunately, the boy had seen not enough to afford Dewart any semblance of a clue. In the scanty account, however, lay an explanation for the fact that the house had been left with books and papers not adequately cared for, the hasty departure of Alijah and his offspring leaving him no time to make preparations for his long visit. There was nothing, indeed, to show that Alijah meant to remain away; but it must have been in his mind that he might do so, however little he took with him. Dewart took up the book again and leafed rapidly through it, re-reading portions here and there, and in this fashion coming upon a further cryptic entry which he had missed because it was lost in the midst of a paragraph setting forth in some detail a visit the child had made to Arkham in the company of the Indian, Quamis. 'It puzzled me no little to discover that everywhere we were treated with great respect and marked fear; the tradesmen were subservient beyond what I had thought tradesmen ought to be, and even Quamis was not troubled as the Indians sometimes are in the streets of towns. Once or twice I overheard beldames whispering to each other in hushed voices, and caught the name "Billington" so uttered, in accents which filled me with concern that it should not be a good name, for all that these ladies would take it so in mistrust and doubt, which were spoken in accents too plain to be mistook, least of all by me, though it may seem, as Quamis said to me on the way home, that I am the victim of my imaginings and my own fears.'

So, then, Old Billington was 'feared' or disliked, and everyone connected with him in any way likewise. This additional discovery put Dewart almost into a fever of anticipation; his quest was so different from the usual genealogical adventure that it delighted him; here was

15

mystery, here was something deep, unfathomable, something out of the routine ken; and, fed by this taste of the mystery, Dewart was stirred and stimulated with the excitement of the chase.

He turned eagerly to the oddments of papers and documents, but was soon conscious of sharp disappointment, for most of them appeared to be in reference to building materials and settlements therefor, and in some cases were statements for books which had been purchased by Alijah Billington from dealers in London, Paris, Prague, and Rome. He had reached almost his nadir of disappointment when he chanced upon a document penned in a crabbed hand, and only in part legible, which bore the arresting heading, *Of Evill Sorceries done in New-England of Daemons in no Humane Shape.* This appeared to have been copied from an account of which the original was not at hand, and it was plain, that not all the original had been copied, and not all the sentences copied were any longer legible. Yet, on the whole, the document was legible enough, and, with some considerable pains, Dewart could piece it out. He read it slowly, with much halting and doubt, and was fascinated by its contents to such an extent that he took up pen and paper and began laboriously to copy it. It began, by the evidence, in the middle of the original.

'But, not to speak at too great Length upon so Horrid a matter, I will add onlie what is commonly reported concerning an Happening in New Dunnich, fifty years since, when Mr. Bradford was Governor. 'Tis said, one Richard *Billington,* being instructed partly by Evill Books, and partly by an antient Wonder-Worker amongst ye *Indian* Savages, so fell away from good *Christian* Practice that he not onlie lay'd claim to Immortality in ye flesh, but sett up in ye woods a great Ring of Stones, inside of which he say'd Prayers to ye Divell, Place of Dagon, Namely, and sung certain Rites of Magick abominable by Scripture. This being brought to ye Notice of ye Magistrates, he deny'd all

16

Blasphemous Dealings; but not long after he privately shew'd great Fear about some Thing he had call'd out of ye Sky at Night. There were in that year seven slayings in ye woods near to *Richard Billington's* Stones, those slain being crushed and half-melted in a fashion outside all experience. Upon Talk of a Tryall, *Billington* dropt out of Sight, nor was any clear Word of him ever after heard. Two months from then, by Night, there was heard a Band of *Wampanaug* Savages howling and singing in ye Woods; and it appeared they took down ye Ring of Stones and did much besides. For their head man *Misquamacus*, that same antient Wonder-Worker of whom *Billington* had learnt some of his Sorceries, came shortly into ye town and told Mr. *Bradford* some strange Things: Namely, that *Billington* had done worse Evill than cou'd be well repair'd, and that he was no doubt eat up by what he had call'd out of ye Sky. That there was no Way to send back that Thing he had summon'd, so ye *Wampanaug* wise Man had caught and prison'd it where the Ring of Stones had been.

'They had digg'd down three Ells deep and two across, and had Thither charmed ye Daemon with Spells that they knew; covering it over with' (here followed an illegible line) 'carved with what they call'd ye *Elder Sign*. On this they' (again a few indistinct words) 'digg'd from ye Pit. The old Savage affirm'd this place was on no Account to be disturb'd, lest ye Daemon come loose again which it wou'd if ye flatt Stone with ye *Elder Sign* shou'd get out of Place. On being ask'd what ye Daemon look'd like, *Misquamacus* cover'd his Face so that onlie ye Eyes look'd out, and then gave a very curious and Circumstantiall Relation, saying it was sometimes small and solid, like a great Toad ye Bigness of many Ground-Hogs, but sometimes big and cloudy, with no Shape, though with a Face which had Serpents grown from it.

'It had ye Name *Ossadagowah*, which signifi'd' (this was rewritten to 'signifys') 'ye child of *Sadogowah*, ye

17

which is held to be a Frightfull Spirit spoke of by antients as come down from ye Stars and being formerly worship in Lands to ye North. Ye *Wampanaugs* and ye *Nansets* and *Nahrigansets* knew how to draw It out of ye Heavens but never did so because of ye exceeding great Evilness of It. They knew also how to catch and prison It, tho' they cou'd not send It back whence It came. It was declar'd that ye old Tribes of *Lamah,* who dwell under ye Great Bear and were antiently destroy'd for their Wickedness, knew how to manage It in all Ways. Many upstart Men pretended to a Knowledge of such and divers other Outer Secrets, but none in these parts cou'd give any Proof of truly having ye aforesaid Knowledge. It was said by some that *Ossadogowah* often went back to ye Sky from choice without any sending, but that he cou'd not come back unless Summon'd.

'This much ye antient Wizard *Misquamacus* told to Mr. *Bradford,* and even after, a great Mound in ye Woods near ye Pond southwest of New Dunnich hath been straitly lett alone. Ye Tall Stone is these Twenty yrs. gone, but ye Mound is mark'd by ye Circumstance, that nothing, neither grass nor brush, will grow upon it. Grave men doubt that ye evill *Billington* was eat up as ye Savages believe, by what he call'd out of Heaven, notwithstanding certain Reports of ye idle, of his being since seen in divers places. Ye Wonder-Worker *Misquamacus* told that he mistrusted not but that *Billington* had been taken; he wou'd not say that he had been eat up by It, as others among ye Savages believ'd, but he affirm'd that *Billington* was no longer on this Earth, whereat God be prais'd.'

Appended to this curious document was a note, evidently hastily scrawled: 'See the Rev. Ward Phillips, *Thau. Prod.*' Dewart rightly supposed that this reference was to a book on the shelves, and without delay carried his lamp over to the shelves and began to scrutinize the titles there. These were of a remarkable diversity, and most of them were utterly unfamiliar to him. There were Lully's *Ars Magna et Ultima,* Fludd's *Clavis Alchimiae,* the *Liber Ivonis,* Albertus Magnus, Artephous' *Key of Wisdom,* the Comte d'Erlette's *Cultes des Goules,* Ludvig Prinn's *De Vermis Mysteriis,* and many other tomes hoary with age, having to do with philosophy, thaumaturgy, demonology, cabalistics, mathematics, and the like, among them several sets of Paracelsus and Hermes Trismogistus, which bore the marks of much usage. In this fascination with these titles, and his resolute determination to refrain from drawing them out one by one and examine them, it was some time before Dewart discovered the volume he sought, but eventually he came to it, pushed well into a corner at the far end of a shelf some distance removed from where he had been sitting.

It was entitled *Thaumaturgical Prodigies in the New-English Canaan,* by the Rev. Ward Phillips, described on the title-page as 'Pastor of the Second Church in Arkham in the Massachusetts-Bay.' The volume was clearly a reprint of an earlier book, for its date was Boston, 1801. It was by no means a slim volume, and Dewart guessed that the Rev. Ward Phillips, in common with many men of the cloth, had been unable to refrain from sermonizing while he developed his theses. There were no book marks of any kind, and, since the hour was drawing on towards midnight, Dewart did not look with enthusiasm upon the prospect of paging through a volume which was printed still with the long *s* and all the other typographical obsolescences of that time. Instead, he hit upon the reasonable assumption that, if Alijah Billington had used the volume to any great extent, he might have cracked the spine at those places where he was wont to open it. He therefore carried the book and the lamp back to the table, and, depositing the lamp, he set the book flat upon its worn leather spine and allowed it to fall open, which, once he had shaken it a little, it did readily enough, at a place approximately two-thirds of the way through the book.

It was printed in an imitation of black letter, and, while strange to the eye, was not as difficult to read as had been the document Dewart had just completed. Moreover, a scrawl along the page—*Compare Nar. of Rich. Billington*—indicated the desired passage beyond any question. It was not long, though episodic in nature, being preceded by nothing specifically pertinent, nor followed by anything pertaining, the Rev. Ward Phillips having taken the opportunity thereafter to indict a short sermon on the 'evill of consorting with Daemons, Familiars, and such ilk.' The passage itself, however, was curiously disturbing.

'But in respect of Generall Infamy, no Report more terrible hath come to Notice, than of what Goodwife *Doten,* Relict of *John Doten* of *Duxbury* in the Old Colonies, brought out of the Woods near Candelmas of 1787. She affirm'd, and her good neighbours likewise, that it had been borne to her, and took oath that she did not know by what manner it had come upon her, for it was neither Beast nor Man but like a monstrous Bat with human face. It made no sound but look'd at all and sundry with baleful eyes. There were those who swore that it bore a frightful resemblance to the Face of one long dead, one *Richard Bellingham* or *Bollinghan* who is affirm'd to have vanished utterly after consort with Daemons in the country of New Dunnich. The horrible Beast-Man was examined by the Court of Azzizes and the which then burnt by Order of the High-Sherif on the 5th of June in the year 1788.'

Dewart re-read this passage several times; it contained certain implications, though none came clearly. In any ordinary circumstances, those implications might have been missed; but, read immediately after what Alijah had labelled the 'Billington Nar.,' the occurrence of the name 'Richard Bellingham or Bollinghan' pointed unmistakably to the parallel with Richard Billington. Unfortunately, however much Dewart's imagination was stimulated, he was unable to conjure up any kind of explanation for the riddle; he presumed that it might possibly be the suggestion of the Rev. Ward Phillips that 'one Richard Bellingham,' supposing he were identical with Richard Billington, had not been destroyed —'Eat up by what he had call'd out of Heaven'—as popular superstition had believed, but had taken himself and his evil practices off into the deeper woods near Duxbury and there perpetuated himself in a secondary line which had ultimately spawned the horror of which the minister had written. On the other hand, the period in which Goodwife Doten had brought forth her changeling was less than a century after the notorious Witchcraft Trials, and it might well be presumed that the superstitions of that time still lingered among the credulous people, clerical as well as lay, who then lived in the country around Duxbury and 'New Dunnich,' which, surely, must be the place known as Dunwich, and thus in the neighbourhood.

Excited and further stimulated to increasing investigations, Dewart sought his bed and there lapsed at once into a sleep much troubled by curious dreams of strange creatures, serpentine and bat-like, which occupied his nighted hours in a fashion he had suspected they might. Yet he slept untroubled, save for one hour in the night when he awoke and lay for a few moments firm in the conviction that he was being watched *from above,* a fancy he had no trouble in dismissing for renewed sleep.

In the morning, considerably exhilarated by his sleep, Ambrose Dewart set out to discover what he could of his ancestor, Alijah, from sources other than his own library. He drove into Arkham which, as an urban centre, he never failed to compare with certain old villages and towns of England, taking much pleasure in the clustering gambrel roofs with the haunted gable rooms, the fan-lighted doorways, and the narrow byways along the Miskatonic, leading from hidden streets into long-forgotten courtyards. He commenced his search at the Library of Miskatonic University, where he sought the carefully treasured volumes of the Arkham *Advertiser* and the Arkham *Gazette* of a century ago.

The morning was bright and clear, and Dewart had all time at his disposal. In many respects, Dewart was a confirmed putterer; he entered into every quest with great zeal, though he seldom saw many of them through. He arranged himself in a well-lit corner, with a reading-table all to himself, and began to go leisurely through the newspapers of his great-great-grandfather's day, which were filled with many curious items which caught his attention and were responsible for several divagations from his quest. He went through several months of papers before he came upon the name of his ancestor, and then it was by accident, for, while he had been seeking in the news-columns, he found it instead beneath a communication to the editor, which was curt and rude.

'Sir: I am appriz'd of a notice in y^r paper by one John Druven, Esq., of a sartain book by the Rev. Ward Phillips of Arkham, which speaks of the said book in terms of praise. I realize it is the custom to heap fine words on men of the cloath, but John Druven, Esq. cou'd have done the Rev. Ward Phillips a greater sarvice by point'g out that there things in existence better left alone and kept from the common speach. Y^r Serv't., Alijah Billington.'

Dewart immediately sought a reply to this communication, and found it in the paper of the following week.

'Sir: 'Tis said the protestant, Alijah Billington, knows whereof he writes. He hath read the book, and I am oblig'd to him and am thus twice his obt. Serv't. in the Name of God. Rev. Ward Phillips.'

There was no further word from Alijah, though for many weeks' issues thereafter, Dewart scrutinized the papers carefully for any communication. The Rev. Ward Phillips, for all the sermonizing in his book, was evidently of no less spirit than Alijah Billington. Thereafter, for some time, there was no mention of the name Billington, and it was not until several hours had gone by—and several years of both the *Advertiser* and the *Gazette,* also—that further notice of the name passed beneath Dewart's eye. This time it was but a brief item of news.

'The High-Sherif has serv'd notice on Alijah Billington in his home off the Aylesbury Pike to cease and desist from the business in which he is engag'd at night, and to abate in particular the noises thereof. Squire Billington has made application to be heard by the Court of the County in its session at Arkham next month.'

Nothing further, then, until Alijah Billington appeared before the Magistrates.

'The accus'd Alijah Billington depos'd that he was engag'd in no business at night, that he did not make noises or cause noises to be made, that he abided by the laws of the Commonwealth, and defy'd anyone to prove otherwise. He presented himself as the victim of superstitious persons who sought to cause him trouble, and who did not understand that he liv'd alone since the death of his lamented wife sev'n yrs. ago. He wou'd not permit the Indian, Quamis, his servant, to be call'd up for testimony. He several times call'd forth and demanded that his accuser be brought to face him or to come up and face him, but it was remark'd that the plaintiff was either reluctant or unwilling to so appear, and, none coming, the said Alijah Billington appear'd vindicated and was order'd to disregard the Notice serv'd on him by the High-Sherif.'

It was plain that the 'noises' referred to by the boy, Laban, in his daybook were no figment of his imagination. This account, however, again suggested that those who had lodged complaint against Alijah Billington were afraid of facing him; there was about this suggestion something more than the ordinary reluctance of trouble-makers to stand up before the object of their mischief. If the boy had heard the noises, and the

23

plaintiff also; then manifestly others had also heard them; yet no one would so state, even to the extent of admitting to hearing noises, with imputing them to Alijah Billington. Plainly Billington was held in some awe, if not fear; he was a forthright, fearless man himself, who did not hesitate to be aggressive, particularly in his own defence. Dewart thought this commendable enough, but he was all the more titillated by the increasing mystery. He felt that the matter of the noises would grow in proportion, rather than be now lost to the papers, and so, indeed, it was.

Scarcely a month later, there appeared in the *Gazette* an impertinent letter from one John Druven, presumably the same gentleman who had reviewed the Rev. Ward Phillips' book, and who might understandably enough have taken sufficient umbrage at Alijah Billington's curt criticism of his notice to interest himself in turn in Billington's troubles with the High-Sheriff.

'Sir: Having occasion to take a walking journey West and North-West of Arkham this day week I was caught by darkness in the woodland in the vicinity of the Aylesbury Pike, in that region known as Billington's Wood, and while endeavouring to make my way from there, I became aware not long after darkness had fallen, of a most hideous din, the nature of which I find myself unable to explain, seem'g to come from the direction of the swamp beyond the house of Alijah Billington, Gent. I listen'd for some time to the aforementioned clamour, and was much distress'd thereby, for more than once it appear'd to bear a mark'd resemblance to the cries of some creature in pain or sickness, and had I known in which direction to pursue my way, I wou'd have mov'd toward it, so sensible was I of suffering and distress. These noises continu'd for a period of a half hour or a little more, and then subsid'd, after which all was still, and I went on my way. Y^r Obt. Serv't., John Druven.'

Dewart fully expected that this would indeed stimulate his ancestor to a wrathful reply, but the weeks went by, and nothing appeared in the papers. Some opposition to Billington, however, appeared to be in the process of crystallization, for, in the absence of any word from Billington, the Rev. Ward Phillips appeared in the papers with an open letter in which he volunteered to lead a committee of investigation towards the site of the noises with the intention of discovering what made the noises and of putting an end to them forthwith. This was clearly calculated to draw Billington forth, and draw him it did. He ignored both the minister and the reviewer in his reply, which took the form of a public notice:

'Any Person and all Persons discover'd to be Trespassing on the Property known as Billington's Woods, or any adjoining Field or Pasture duly affix'd by Deed to the said Billington's Wood, will be taken up as Trespassors and plac'd under Arrest for Triall. Alijah Billington has this Day appear'd before a Magistrate and deposed that his Property is duly Mark'd Against Trespassing, Hunting, Loitering, and all similar encroachments without Permission.'

This brought forth an immediate goad from the Rev. Ward Phillips, who wrote that it 'wou'd seem, our Neighbour, Alijah Billington, is unwilling that any investigation of the noises be made and desireth that they be contain'd within his ken alone.' He concluded his artful letter by coming out point-blank and asking Alijah Billington why he 'fear'd' to have the noises and their source either investigated or ended.

Alijah, however, was not to be put down by mere artfulness. He replied soon after that he had no intention of being put upon by 'all and sundry'; he had no reason to believe that the self-appointed 'Rev. Ward Phillips, or his protégé, John Druven, Gent.' were in any way qualified to conduct such an investigation; and then he lashed out at those who claimed to hear noises. 'As for these Persons, surely it is not amiss to inquire of what they did out at this hour of the Night, when decent Persons are abed, or at least, within their own walls, and not gadding about in the Country under cover of Darkness, God knows after what pleasures or pursuits? They offer no evidence that they heard noises. The deponent, Druven, declaims loudly that he heard noises; but he makes no mention of any other accompanying him. There were those, too, scarce a hundred years ago, who fancied they heard voices and accus'd innocent men and women who were thereupon put to death most horribly as Warlocks and Witches; their evidence was no more. Is the deponent well enough appriz'd of country sounds in the night-time to distinguish between what he calls the "cries of some creature in pain" and the bellowing of a bull, or the lowing of a cow in search of a lost calf, or sundry other sounds of similar Nature? It is better that he and his ilk mind their tongues, and let their ears not betray them, nor look upon that which is not meant by God to be seen.'

This was an ambiguous letter, indeed. Billington had not previously called upon God to witness for him, and his letter, though in some respects pointed, yet had the marks of one written in haste, and without considered judgment. In short, Billington had let himself lie open to attack, and he must expect to be attacked, as he was, directly, by both the Rev. Ward Phillips, and John Druven.

The minister wrote, almost as curtly as Billington had originally written, that he was 'happy indeed, and I thank God, to observe that the man, Billington, doth recognize that there are divers Thing which God did not mean man to see, and I hope onlie that the said Billington has himself not looked upon them.'

John Druven, however, gibed at Alijah. 'Forsooth, I did not know Neighbour Billington kept bulls and cows and calfs, with whose voices the deponent is familiar, hav'g been rais'd among them. Deponent sayeth further he heard no voice of bull or cow or calf in the vicinity of Billington's Woods. Nor of goat nor sheep nor ass, nor any animal familiar to me. And noises there are, it cannot be deny'd, for I heard them, and others like-wise.' And so on, in similar vein.

It might have been expected that Billington would make some kind of reply; but he did not. Nothing further bearing his signature appeared, but three months later the *Gazette* printed a communication from the needling Druven that he had received an invitation to investigate Billington's Wood at his leisure, either by himself, or in company, Billington requiring only that he be formally notified of Druven's intention of so do-ing, so that he could issue orders that he be not molested as a Trespassor. Druven signified his intention of accept-ing Billington's invitation all in good time.

Then for some time, nothing further.

And then a series of sinister paragraphs growing in-creasingly alarming as the weeks went by. The initial news-item was innocuous. It stated only that 'John Dru-ven, Gent., occasionally employ'd by this paper,' had failed to turn in his copy in time to appear in the paper this week, and would presumably have it prepared for next week's issue. 'Next week,' however, the *Gazette* carried a somewhat expanded paragraph saying that John Druven 'could not be found. He was not in his rooms on River Street, and a search is now being made to discover his whereabouts.' The week after that, the *Gazette* disclosed that the missing copy Druven had promised to send in was to be a report on a visit he had made to Billington's house and woods, in the com-pany of the Rev. Ward Phillips and Deliverance Wes-tripp. His companions could testify that they had re-turned from Billington's. But that night, according to his landlady, Druven had set forth from the house. He had not responded to an inquiry as to whither he was going. Asked about their investigation of the noises in Billington's Wood, the Rev. Phillips and Deliverance Westripp could remember nothing, save that their host had been very courteous to them, and had even served them a luncheon prepared by his servant, the Indian,

Quamis. The High-Sheriff was now conducting an investigation into the disappearance of John Druven.

In the fourth week, no further news of John Druven. Likewise in the fifth week.

Silence thereafter, save at the expiration of three months, when it was admitted that the High-Sheriff was no longer carrying on the investigation into John Druven's strange disappearance.

No further word of Billington, either. The whole matter of the noises in Billington's Wood seemed to have been dropped with decisive determination. Neither news columns nor communications column carried so much as Billington's name.

Six months after Druven's disappearance, however, matters occurred with startling rapidity, and Dewart was keenly conscious of the restraint manifest in the papers' handling of the events of that time, events which in his own time would have made exciting headlines. Within a period of three weeks four separate stories occupied the most important place in both the *Gazette* and the *Advertiser*.

The first story concerned the discovery of a badly torn and mangled body on the ocean's edge in the immediate vicinity of the seaport town of Innsmouth at the mouth of the Manuxet River. The body was identified as that of John Druven. 'It is believ'd that Mr. Druven may have gone to sea and sustain'd injuries in the wreck of the vessel on which he travel'd. When found, he was some days dead. He was last known to have been in Arkham half a year ago, and no word of him has been had by anyone since that time. He appears to have undergone severe trialls in body, for his face is uncommon drawn, and many bones are broke.'

The second account concerned Dewart's ancestor, the ubiquitous Alijah Billington. It was made known that Billington and his son, Laban, had departed for a visit with relatives in England.

A week later, the Indian, Quamis, who had served Alijah, 'was desir'd for question'g by the High-Sherif, but cou'd not be found. Two bailiffs went to the house of Alijah Billington, but found no one there. The house being lock'd and seal'd, they cou'd not enter without warrant, which they had not.' Inquiry among the then Indian population remaining in the Dunwich country to the northwest of Arkham elicited no further information; indeed, the Indians knew nothing of Quamis and wished to know nothing, and two of them 'deny'd that such a Person as Quamis either came from among their number or exist'd at all.'

Finally, the High-Sheriff released a fragment of a letter which the late Druven had begun to write on the evening of his strange and inexplicable disappearance now approximately seven months before. It was addressed to the Rev. Ward Phillips, and bore the 'mark of haste,' according to the account in the *Gazette*. The letter had been discovered by the landlady and given to the High-Sheriff, who admitted to its existence only now. The *Gazette* printed it.

'To the Rev. Ward Phillips
Baptist Church
French Hill, in Arkham
'My Esteem'd Friend,
'I have been come over with the feel'g of grave strangeness to such degree that it wou'd seem my memory of the events we witness'd this afternoon is impair'd to fad'g. I find it impossible to account for this, and in addition to it I am impell'd now to think more of our erstwhile host, the redoubtable Billington, as if I must go to him, and as if the wonder whether he might by some magick means have put something into the food of which we partook to impair memory were needless unkind. Do not think ill of me, my good Friend, but I am hard beset to recall what it was we saw at the circle of stones in the wood, and with each passing instant, methinks memory grows more dim. . . .'

Here the letter ended; there was no more. The *Gazette* had printed it as found, nor did the editor presume to draw any conclusions therefrom. The High-

Sheriff had said only that Alijah Billington would be asked questions on his return, and that was all. Subsequently, there was a notice of the internment of the unfortunate Druven, and after that, a letter from the Rev. Ward Phillips to say that members of his parish living in that outlying country near Billington's Wood had reported that there were no longer noises to be heard in the night, now that Alijah Billington had taken his departure for foreign shores.

There was no further mention of Billington in six months more of the papers, and at that point Dewart ceased to look. Despite the fascination which this research held for him, his eyes were tiring; moreover, the hour was now mid-afternoon; he had completely neglected his luncheon-hour, and, though he was not hungry, Dewart thought it best to desist from abusing his eyes. He was somewhat bewildered by the accounts he had read. In one sense, he was disappointed; he had expected to come upon something of greater clarity, but in everything he had read, there was a tenuous vagueness, an almost mystic haziness, even less tangible than those cryptic fragments found in the documents in what remained of Alijah Billington's library. The newspaper reports presented little of a definite nature of themselves. Indeed, there was only the circumstantial support of the boy, Laban's, daybook to prove that the accusers of Alijah Billington did actually hear noises in Billington's Wood at night. Apart from this, Billington was painted as at least half a rascal, irascible, forthright, almost bullying, and not afraid to face his detractors; he had emerged from every encounter rather well, though the Rev. Ward Phillips had made a telling point or two. There could be no doubt that the book to the review of which Alijah had taken such a rude exception was the *Thaumaturgical Prodigies in the New-English Canaan*; and, while there was nothing admissible as evidence in a modern court, there was a very strong coincidence to be noted in the fact that Alijah's most irritating critic, John Druven, should have disappeared so strangely. Moreover, Druven's unfinished letter posed certain startling questions. The inference was plain that Alijah had put something into the repast to make his unwelcome visitors—the 'investigating committee'—forget what it was that they had seen; ergo, they had seen something to substantiate the veiled charges made by Druven and the Rev. Ward Phillips. There was something more inherent in that fragment of a letter—'as if I must go to him.' It was disturbing for Dewart to reflect upon this, for it suggested that by some means Billington had drawn the most acidulous of his critics back to him, and ultimately effected his death, after first bringing about his removal from the scene.

Though these were but speculations, nevertheless, Dewart occupied himself with them all the way back to the house in the woods, arriving at which, he sought out again the papers he had read on the previous night and pored over them for some time, trying by some means to effect a relationship between the Richard Billington of the document and the feared Alijah—not a relationship of kin, for he had no doubt that they were of one and the same line, several generations apart; but rather a connection in substance between the incredible events chronicled in the document, and the accounts in the Arkham weeklies, for it seemed inescapable to him, after some careful consideration, that such a connection existed, if it were only in the coincidence that in both accounts, separated by more than a century in time, and by some miles in space, the one having occurred at 'New Dunnich' which was presumably now Dunwich (unless the entire region had been once so named), and the other at Billington's Wood, there was mention of a 'circle of stones,' which undeniably brought to mind the Druidic fragments roughly circling the stone tower in the bed of that dried-up tributary to the Miskatonic.

Dewart prepared himself several sandwiches, slipped an orange and a flashlight into the pockets of his jacket, and set out in the late afternoon sunlight to skirt the swamp and make his way to the tower, which he entered, and which he began immediately to examine anew. There was on the interior, spiralling up along the side, an extremely narrow and crude stairway of stone, and, with some misgivings, Dewart mounted it, observing all along the way, a kind of primitive but impressive decoration in the nature of bas-relief, which he soon saw was a single design repeated as a chain for the entire length of the stair, which ended finally in a little platform so close to the roof of the tower that Dewart could scarcely crouch upon it. The light in his hand showed him that the bas-relief which was carved into the stones along the stairs also appeared on the platform, and he bent to scrutinize it more closely, thus discovering it to be an intricate pattern of concentric circles and radiating lines, which, the more attentively it was gazed at, offered a perplexing maze to the eye in that it seemed at one moment to be of such an appearance, and in the next appeared to change inexplicably. Dewart directed his light upward.

It had been apparent to him in his previous examination of the tower, that some carving had been made in that portion of the roof which had seemed of manifestly more recent origin, but he now saw that but one stone bore a decoration, and that this was a large flat block of what seemed to be limestone, corresponding almost exactly in size with the platform on which he crouched. Its decoration, however, did not follow the motif of the bas-relief figures, but was, rather, in the rough shape of a star, in the centre of which there appeared to be a caricature of a single giant eye; but it was not an eye, rather a broken lozenge in shape with certain lines suggestive of flames or perhaps a solitary pillar of flame.

The design meant no more to Dewart than the pattern of the bas-relief, but what did interest him was the observation that the cement holding this block in place had succumbed in large part to the ravages of the weather, and it occurred to him that a little adroit and skilful chipping away of what cement remained might free the stone, and afford an opening in the side of the conical roof. Indeed, as he played his light over the ceiling, it was apparent that the tower had originally been constructed with an opening, which had been later closed by the addition of this flat stone, which was singular in that it was less rough than the other stones in the building, and had a greyish cast, though this might well be due to its newness as well as in part to the darkness inside the tower.

As he crouched there, Dewart was convinced that the tower should be restored to its original structure; indeed, the more he contemplated this restoration, the more obsessed he became, until he was determined beyond question to effect the desired change, and remove the block above the platform, and thus afford himself enough room to stand up. He swept the earth below with his light, and, seeing there a fragment of stone which might be utilized as a chipping tool, he descended carefully and got it, testing the feel of it. Then he returned to the platform and considered how best he might effect his purpose without danger to himself; the stone was not so large that he could not at least direct it past the platform when it was ready to fall, but it was heavy enough so that he could not hope to sustain its full weight. He braced himself against the wall there, and began carefully to chip away, the light stuck awkwardly in his pocket, and in a short while it was evident to him that he would first have to chip away that portion nearest him, so that the block, in falling, would tend to fall away from the wall and him, and off the edge of the platform to the earthen floor below.

He bent assiduously to his task, and in half an hour, the stone fell away, as he had planned it, and, guided by him, slipped past the platform to the floor below. Dewart stood up and found himself looking out across the marsh to eastward, and so for the first time saw that the tower was in line with the house, for, directly across the open space of the marsh and the trees beyond, the sunlight glinted on a window of his home. Which window this could be he wondered briefly; he had not caught sight of the tower from any opening, but then, he had not sought it; and the window, judging by its expanse, could be none other than the window of coloured glass in the study, through which he had never looked.

Dewart could not imagine to what use the tower had been put. As he stood there now, he could support his hands on the frame of that opening; for he stood out in part over the roof of the tower, even above the peak of it, and his view was best of the heavens. It might have been constructed by some early astronomer; assuredly it was ideal for use in watching the heavenly bodies wheeling overhead. The stones of the conical roof, Dewart noticed, were fully as thick as those of the walls, something over a foot—possibly fifteen inches; and the fact that the roof had stood unshaken through all these years gave testimony of the skill of that early architect who had built this tower and perhaps other buildings and gone unsung into history. Yet, an astronomical explanation for the tower's existence was not wholly satisfactory; for the fact was that the tower rose up not on a hill, or even on a knoll of any proportion, but only on an island, or what had once been an island, a slight rise in the earth, and the land sloped down towards it it from three sides, sloping away from it only on the gentle declivity which descended very gradually to the Miskatonic some distance through the woods, and it was only by accident that the tower commanded the heavens, for no trees grew in the immediate proximity, nor indeed did much brush or grass of any kind. Even so, the horizon was contained by the trees of the encroaching slopes, so that the stars were not at their best visibility until some time past the hour of their rising, and were again not visible for a brief time before their setting, which was not a condition ideally conducive to star-study.

After a while, Dewart descended the stairs once more, busied himself briefly in moving the stone off to one side, and made his way out of the arched doorway, which offered no barrier of any kind to shut out wind and weather, a circumstance which made the closing of the roof-opening all the more curious.

He did not ponder this long, however, for the sunlight was drawing away as the sun descended behind the belt of trees, but, munching his remaining sandwich, set out along the way he had come, again walking along the edge of the marsh and up the rise to his house, the four great frontal pillars, squarely built into the walls of the house, showing whitely in the gathering twilight. He was somewhat exhilarated, as he always was at progress in any kind of research he undertook; however little he had this day discovered that was concrete and capable of but one interpretation, he had uncovered many speculations, and much of interest about native lore and legend as well as about his ancestor, the foresighted Alijah, who had set Arkham by the ears, so to speak, and left such a mystery behind him that few since his time remained to equal it. He had actually amassed a great many details, and could not be sure that they represented different parts of the same pattern, or parts of different designs.

Arriving at the house, he was tired. He resisted the temptation to delve further into his great-great-grandfather's books, knowing he must consider his eyes, and instead set about methodically to plot his further researches, quite as if these hundreds of ancient books were not available to him. Comfortably ensconced in the study, with a fire again going on the hearth, Dewart went over in his mind all the aspects of the research in progress with a view to determining which of them offered the most ready avenue of further discovery. He thought several times of the missing servant, Quamis, and presently realized that there existed also a kind of parallel between the name of this servant and the name of the Wonder-Worker of the older document—Misquamacus. Quamis or Quamus—the boy had written it both ways—included in the latter spelling actually two of the four syllables of the Indian wise man's name, and, while it was true that many Indian names were similar, it was quite likely that family resemblances in nomenclature were reasonably consistent.

This train of thought presently suggested to him that there might still be alive in the back country in the hills around Dunwich relatives or descendants of Quamis; that he had been disavowed by his own people a century ago and more did not trouble Dewart. A man put out of mind a hundred years ago might well fare more honestly remembered now than some other over whom the gloss of time and the romance of years had fallen to becloud the individual and his character. He might well pursue this line of investigation, weather permitting, on the morrow; and, having decided this, Dewart took himself off to bed.

He slept well, though on two occasions during the night he stirred restlessly and woke and was again conscious of the conviction that the very walls watched him where he lay.

In mid-morning, after he had taken time to answer a few letters which had lain waiting his leisure for several days, he set out for Dunwich. The sky was overcast, and a light east wind blew, presaging rain; as a result of this change in the weather, the wooded hills and their stone-crowned tops which were indigenous to the Dunwich country seemed dark and sinister. In that region, little travelled because it was somewhat away from the beaten track, and because there was to those who knew of it a lurking suggestion of decay about the deserted houses, the roads often narrowed to mere ruts, with the weeds and brambles and grasses, luxuriant and wild, pressing over the stone walls close upon the byways. Dewart had not gone far, before he was keenly conscious of the strangeness of this country, differing sharply from even the ancient gambrel-roofed town of Arkham; for, in contrast to the rolling hills of the country along the Aylesbury Pike out of Arkham, the Dunwich hills were broken by strangely deep ravines and gorges, crossed by rickety bridges, which had the aspect of centuried age, and the hills themselves were curiously crowned with stones which, though much overgrown offered certain suggestive evidence that the crowning formations were the work of men, perhaps of decades, perhaps even of centuries past. Seen now against the louring clouds, the hills more than once presented oddly malign faces to the lone traveller in his car creeping carefully along the rutted roads and across the ricket bridges.

Dewart observed with a queer tightening of his scalp that the very foliage seemed to flourish unnaturally, and, though he interpreted this as evidence of nature's reclaiming of the land so evidently abandoned by those who owned it, it was nevertheless strange that the vines should be so much longer, the scrub growth so much sturdier—even as they were on some of the remoter slopes of his own land. Moreover, the Miskatonic, winding serpent-like through the country, though Dewart had driven away from it, now rose up before him, its dark waters doubly dark in this region, and offered strange vistas of rocky meadows and lush marshes, where the bull-frogs still piped, despite the season.

He had driven perhaps an hour over terrain which was utterly alien to that he had come to know as typically eastern American, when he arrived at the cluster of houses which was Dunwich, though no sign survived to identify it, most of the dwellings being deserted and in various stages of ruin. The broken-steepled church offered what appeared to Dewart, after a quick scrutiny, the only mercantile establishment in the settlement, and he accordingly drove towards it and parked alongside the walk. Two shabby old men leaned up against the building, and, taking in their appearance of mental and physical degeneracy and inbreeding, Dewart addressed himself to them.

'Does either of you men know any Indian stock left around here?'

One of the old men detached himself from the building and came shambling over towards the car. He had narrowed eyes, sunk deeply in leathery skin, and his hands, Dewart noted, were almost claw-like. Dewart assumed that he had come to answer his question, and a little impatiently, leaned forward, so that his inquiring face was thrust clear of the shadow of the roof.

He was disagreeably surprised when his would-be informant started and fell back.

'Luther!' he called in a quavering voice to the oldster behind him. 'Luther! Come hyar!' And, the other scuffling up to peer over his shoulder, he pointed to Dewart. 'Ye 'member thet picter Mis' Giles shown us thet day,' he continued excitedly. 'It's him, sure es tarnation! He looks more'n haff like thet picter naow, dun't he? It's the time, Luther, it's the time they tell abaout—when he comes back, thet other'n 'll come back, too.'

The other oldster tugged at his jacket. 'Wait naow, Seth. Dun't ye be too hasty. Ask him fer the sign.'

'The sign!' exclaimed Seth. 'Hev ye got the sign, Stranger?'

Dewart, who had never in his existence encountered creatures like these, was repelled. It required a conscious effort to prevent himself from showing distaste; he could not keep himself from betraying stiffness.

'I'm looking for traces of the old Indian families,' he said shortly.

'Hain't no Injuns left,' said the man Luther.

Dewart ventured a brief explanation. He had not expected to find Indians. But he thought that he might discover a family or two which had come down from intermarriage. He explained in the simplest words he could find, and was uneasily conscious of the fixed stare of Seth.

'What were thet feller's name again, Luther?' he asked suddenly.

'It were Billington, thet's what.'

'Yore name Billington?' asked Seth boldly.

'My great-great-grandfather was Alijah Billington,' answered Dewart. 'Now, about those families . . .'

He had not sooner identified himself than both the old men underwent a complete change in manner; from simply curious individuals, they became almost fawning and subservient.

'Ye take the Glen rud, and ye stop at the first haouse this side o' Spring Glen—name o' Bishop—the Bishops got Injun blood and maybe suthin' more ye ain't axed abaout. An' ye'd better git away from there afore the whipperwills start a-talkin' an' the frogs begin to call, er ye'll be settin' lost somew'eres an' ye'll hear strange things a-rushin' an' a-talkin' in the air. Bein' o' Billington blood, maybe ye wun't mind, but I'm baound to tell ye 's if ye axed me.'

'Which is the Spring Glen road?' asked Dewart.

'Ye take the secunt turn, an' ye take accaount o' whar the rud leads tew, an' dun't go tew far. It's the first haouse ye come tew this side o' Spring Glen. If Mis' Bishop's to hum, she'll likely tell ye whut ye wunt to know.'

Dewart was desirous of driving away at once; he was disturbed by the uncouthness of these oldsters, who were not only physically unclean, but bore the stigmata of inbreeding, with queer, malformed ears and eye-sockets; yet he was struck by increasing curiosity as to where these old men had come upon the name of Billington.

'You mentioned Alijah Billington,' he said. 'What is it they say about him?'

'No offence meant, no offence a-tall,' said Luther hastily. 'Yew jist set on fer the rud to the Glen.'

Dewart showed some impatience.

Seth inched forward a little and explained apologetically. 'Yew see, yer great-great-grandfather was high-thought-of araound hyar, an' Mis' Giles had a picter uv him drawed by somebody she knew, an' ye look suthin' like him, thet ye dew. They allus sed Billington blood'd be back tew thet haouse in the woods.'

With this Dewart had to be content; he felt that these oldsters did not trust him, but he was not apprehensive about the directions they had given him. He made the turn into the Spring Glen road without trouble, and, driving up into the hills under the ever darkening sky, he came ultimately to the spring which gave the glen its name, and there turned, knowing he had come to the turn for the Bishop house. After a little trouble, he found a low house with faded white siding; he thought it at first to be of Greek revival architecture, but realized that it was far older when he came close to it. This was the Bishop house, for on one of the gate-posts, only half-legible for weather wear, the name Bishop was crudely scrawled. He made his way up a weed-grown path, walking gingerly over a low porch, much worn and weathered, and knocked on the door, filled with misgivings, for the place wore such an air of desertion that it did not seem that anyone could be living in it.

But a voice answered him—the old, cracked voice of a woman—and bade him enter and make his business known.

He opened the door, and immediately an almost nauseating stench assailed him; moreover, the room into which he walked was not only dark because of the day's darkness, but because the windows were shuttered, and no light burned. It was only by the circumstance that he left the door partly ajar behind him that he made out the form of an old crone hunched over in a rocking chair; her white hair almost shone in the darkness of the room.

'Set, stranger,' she said.

'Mrs. Bishop?' he asked.

She acknowledged that she was Mrs. Bishop, and, a little too eagerly, he launched into the tale of his quest for the descendants of the old Indian families of the region. He had been told that she might have Indian blood.

'Yew heard right, sir. The blood uv the Narragansetts flows in my veins, an' afore them, the Wampanaugs, who were more'n Indians.' She chuckled. 'Ye hev the look uv a Billington, ye hev.'

'So I've been told,' he said dryly. 'That is my stock.'

'Of a Billington cum-a-lookin' an' a-peerin' for Indian blood. Are yew lookin' fer Quamis, then?'

'Quamis!' exclaimed Dewart, startled. Immediately he conjectured that somehow the tale of Billington and his servant, Quamis, was known to Mrs. Bishop.

'Aye, ye start an' ye jump, Stranger. But yew needn't tew look fer Quamis because he never cum back, and he ain't never comin' back. He went out there, an' he ain't never wantin' tew come back here agin.'

'What do you know about Alijah Billington?' he asked abruptly.

'Yew may well ask. I know nothing but what was handed down from my folks. Alijah knew more'n mortal man.' She cackled with muttered laughter. 'He knew more'n man was made to know. Magick an' Elder rote. A wise man was Alijah Billington; ye'er uv good blood fer certain things. But ye'll not do like Alijah did, an' mind—yew leave the stone an' keep the door sealed an' locked so thet them from Outside can't git back.'

As the old woman talked, a strange sense of apprehension began insidiously to make itself felt in Ambrose Dewart. The enterprise upon which he had embarked with so much zest, removed now from the pale of old books and newspapers to the realm of the mundane, in so far as anything in this ancient hamlet could be so considered, began to take on an aspect not alone of the sinister, but of nameless evil. The old beldame shrouded in the self-imposed darkness of the room—a darkness which adequately concealed her features from Dewart, yet permitted her to see him and, like the two

41

oldsters in the village, detect his resemblance to Alijah Billington—began to seem daemonic; her cackling laughter was obscene and horrible, a thin sound, like to the chittering of bats; the words she spoke with such a casual manner seemed to Dewart, who was ordinarily unimaginative, fraught with strange and terrible meaning, which, though it was his nature to refute, he found difficulty in viewing prosaically. As he sat listening, he told himself that it was to be expected that queer, otherworldly beliefs and superstitions would be rife in such out-of-the-way places as these Massachusetts hills; yet there was no aura of simple superstition about Mrs. Bishop, there was rather a conviction of hidden knowledge, and in addition, a most disturbing sense of secret, almost contemptuous superiority on the part of the old woman.

'What was it they suspected my great-great-grandfather of?'

'Yew doan't know?'

'Was it sorcery?'

'Conniving with the Devil?' She tittered again. 'It was wus'n that. It was suthin' nobody can tell. But It didn't git Alijah when it was a-roamin' the hills an' a-screamin' an' all thet hellish music, too. Alijah called It an' It came: Alijah sent It an' It went. It went where It's a-waitin an' a-lurkin' an' a-keepin' Its time this hundred-year for the door tew be set open agin, so It can come out an' go among the hills agin.'

The old woman's oblique references had the sound of a familiar's description; Dewart knew a smattering of sorcery and demonology. And yet, there was something strangely alien to even this in her talk.

'Mrs. Bishop, did you ever hear of Misquamacus?'

'He was the great wise man uv the Wampanaugs. I heard my grandfather tell uv him.'

So much, then, was at least of legend.

'And this wise man, Mrs. Bishop . . .'

'Oh, ye needn't tew ask. He knew. There was Billingtons in his time, tew, ye know right well. Ain't no need fer me tew tell. But I'm an old woman; 'twon't be long I wun't be on airth much longer; I ain't afear'd tew say it. Ye'll find it in the books.'

'What books?'

'The books yere great-great-gran'father read in; ye'll find it all there. They'll tell ye if ye read 'em right how It answered from the hill an' how It cum out uv the air, right as if 'twas from the stars. But ye'll not do as he did; if ye dew, may Him Who Is Not To Be Named hev maircy on ye? It's a-waitin' up there. It's a-waitin' outside right naow as if 'twere yesterday It was sent back. Ain't no sich thing as *time* fer them things. Ain't no sich thing es space, nuther. I'm a pore woman, I'm an old woman, I wun't be on this airth long any more, but I'm tellin' ye I see the shadows o' them things araound ye where ye set right naow, a-hoverin' an' a-flutterin', jest waiting' an' waitin'. Dun't ye go a-callin' out tew the hills.'

Dewart listened with growing uneasiness, and with something of that phenomenon known as 'crawling flesh.' The old woman herself, the setting, the sound of her voice—all were eerie; despite being enclosed by the walls of this old house, Dewart had an oppressive and foreboding sense of being invaded by the darkness and the brooding mystery of the stone-crowned hills all around; he had a furtive and uncanny conviction of something looking over his shoulder, as if the oldsters from Dunwich had followed him here, and a vast, silent company behind them, and listened to what was being said. Of a sudden, the room seemed alive with presences, and at the instant that Dewart's imagination so trapped him, the old woman's voice faded and gave way to a horrible tittering.

He stood up abruptly.

Some sense of his revulsion must have communicated itself to the old crone, for her tittering stopped immediately, and at once her voice gave forth in a servile whine. 'Dun't ye harm me, Master. I'm an old woman not long fer this airth.'

Even more than before, this manifest evidence that he was feared filled Dewart with a strangely exhilarating alarm. He was not accustomed to servility, and there was something nauseatingly frightful about this fawning attitude, something alien to his nature, and, because he knew it grew not out of knowledge of him, but out of some legendary beliefs regarding old Alijah, there was something doubly repellent about it.

'Where can I find Mrs. Giles?' he asked shortly.

'T'other end o' Dunwich. She lives alone but fer her son, an' he's a wild one, a mite tetched, they dew say.'

He had hardly set foot on the porch before he was conscious that there was rising behind him once more that horrible tittering that was the laughter of Mrs. Bishop. Despite his abhorrence, he stood there for a moment, listening. The tittering subsided, and instead came the sound of mumbled words; but, to Dewart's amazement, the old crone's words were not in English, but in a kind of phonetic language that was infinitely startling in this rankly overgrown valley deep in the hills. He listened, somewhat unnerved, but with a rising curiosity to fix in his memory what it was the old woman mumbled to herself. As nearly as he could determine, the sounds she made were a combination of grunted half-words and aspirates, certainly not in any language with which he was familiar. He made some attempt to transcribe them, writing on the back of an envelope in his pocket, but when he had finished and looked at what he had written, it was clear that this gibberish could not possibly be interpreted, *'N'gai, n'ga'ghaa, shoggog, y'hah, Nyarla-to, Nyarla-totep, Yog-Sotot, n-yah, n-yah.'* The sounds inside went on for some time before silence fell; but they seemed nothing but a repetition and rearrangement of the primal inflections. Dewart gazed at the transcription he had made in utter bafflement; the woman was obviously almost illiterate, superstitious, and credulous; yet there was the suggestion of some foreign language about these curious phoneticisms, and, from what Dewart knew of his earlier college years, he was reasonably certain that they were not of Indian origin.

He reflected somewhat ruefully that, far from learning anything which might help to bring the portrait of his ancestor into focus, he seemed to be plunging deeper and deeper into an eddying swirl of mystery, or rather, of mysteries, for the disjointed conversation of old Mrs. Bishop pointed to hitherto unknown puzzles, none of which seemed to have any other connection save a nebulous one to Alijah Billington, or, at least, to the name of Billington, as if it were a catalytic agent precipitating a shower of memories which yet lacked a central design or intelligence to give the whole meaning.

He folded the envelope carefully to protect his writing, put it back into his pocket, and, now that only silence came from inside to set against the hushing of wind in the trees outside the house, he made his way back to his car and started away, back the road he had come, back through the village, where he was eyed from windows and doorways with wary, half-furtive persistence by dark, silent figures, to where he reasoned Mrs. Giles' house might be. There were three houses which might be said to fit into Mrs. Bishop's general directive of the 'other end' of Dunwich.

He tried the middle one of the three, but, receiving no answer went on to the last of them in the long row which occupied a distance of what would in Arkham pass for three blocks. His approach, however, had not gone unnoticed. He had scarcely turned in to the third house when the large, hunched figure of a man broke from the bushes beside the highway and ran towards the house, bawling lustily.

'Maw! Maw! He's a-comin'.'

The door opened and engulfed him. Dewart, reflecting upon the increasing evidence of decadence and degeneracy in this forsaken hamlet, resolutely followed. The house had no porch; its front face was a bleak, unpainted wall, with a door set in the precise middle of it, less attractive than a barn and almost forbidding in its atmosphere of barrenness and squalor. He knocked.

The door opened and a woman stood there.

'Mrs. Giles?' He tipped his hat.

She paled. He was conscious of a sharp annoyance, but suppressed it in favour of his curiosity.

'I don't mean to frighten you,' he went on. 'I can't help noticing, though, that my appearance seems to frighten Dunwich people. It did Mrs. Bishop, too. She was kind enough to tell me that I resembled someone—my great-great-grandfather, to be frank. She told me you had a picture I might see.'

Mrs. Giles stepped back, her long, narrow face a little less colourless now. Dewart observed from the corner of his eye that the hand which the woman had held under her apron, was clenched upon a tiny figure, which, even in the brief glance he had of it when the draught lifted her apron a little, he identified as akin to the witch charms found in the Black Forest of Germany, and in sections of Hungary and the Balkans: a protective charm.

'Dun't ye let him in, Maw.'

'My son ain't used to strangers,' said Mrs. Giles shortly. 'If ye set a spell, I'll git the picter. It was draw'd a plenty years ago, and it come to me from my father.'

Dewart thanked her and sat down.

She disappeared into an inner room, where her voice was heard in an attempt to soothe her son, whose fright was yet another manifestation of the Dunwich attitude towards him. But perhaps this attitude rose from a general ignorance of all strangers, and applied equally well to any other interloper in this long-forgotten hill country. Mrs. Giles came back and thrust the drawing into his hands.

It was crude, but effective. Even Dewart was startled, for, allowing for the amateurishness of the artist of more than a century ago, it was plain that there was a marked resemblance between him and his great-great-grandfather. Here in this rough sketch were the same square-jawed features, the same steady eyes, the same Roman nose, though Alijah Billington's nose wore a wen on the left side, and his eyebrows were considerably bushier. But then, thought Dewart absorbedly, he was a much older man.

'Ye might be his son,' said Mrs. Giles.

'We had no likeness of him at home,' said Dewart. 'I was curious to see it.'

'Ye kin hev it, if ye like.'

Dewart's impulse was to accept this gift, but he realized that, however little it might mean to her, it had an intrinsic value as a showing-off piece; there was no need for him to have it. He shook his head, still looking at it, taking in every detail of his great-great-grandfather's appearance; then handed it back, thanking her gravely.

Gingerly, with marked hesitation, the overgrown hulk of boy crept into the room and stood at the threshold, poised for instant flight before any manifestation of dislike on Dewart's part. Dewart's glance flickered over him, and he saw that he was no boy, but rather a man of perhaps thirty; the unkempt hair framed a wild face, out of which the eyes looked in fear and fascination at Dewart.

Mrs. Giles stood quietly waiting for him to make the next move; it was obvious that she wished him to be gone; so he got up at once—at which movement the woman's son fled once more into the interior of the house—thanked her again, and left the house, observing that all the time he had been in it, the woman had not once relinquished her hold upon the witch-protection charm or whatever it was to which she clung with such determination.

There was now nothing left for him to do but leave the Dunwich country. He was not loath to do so, however disappointed he had been in his mission, though the sight of his ancestor's portrait as drawn in the old man's own time was at least a partial repayment for his time and effort. But the fact was that his excursion into the Dunwich country had given him an unaccountable feeling of uneasiness, coupled with a kind of physical revulsion which seemed rooted in more than the bad taste the manifest decadence and degeneracy of the region left in his mouth. He could not explain it. The Dunwich people themselves were curiously repellent; it was undeniable, they were like a race unto themselves, with all the stigmata of inbreeding and some curiously different physiological variations—like the oddly flat ears, grown so close to their heads that they might have been attached over a far wider area than normal, and flaring in bat-fashion along the back; and the pale, bulging eyes, almost ichthyic; and the broad, loose mouth, batrachian by suggestion. But it was not alone the Dunwich people, nor the Dunwich country that affected him so disagreeably; it was also something more, something inherent in the very atmosphere of the region, something incredibly old and evil, something that suggested terrible ancient blasphemies and incredible horrors. Fear and terror and horror seemed to become tangible entities in this hidden valley; lust and cruelty and despair seemed to be an inevitable part of life in the Dunwich country; violence and viciousness and perversion suggested themselves as ways of life here; and over everything lay the further conviction of a madness that affected all the people of the region, without regard for age or heritage, an environmental madness which was infinitely more terrible because it carried with it the implication of self-choice. But there was even more than that to Dewart's repulsion; he could not escape the fact that he had been most disagreeably affected by the very obvious fear of him that the natives had shown. However much he might tell himself that it might be a normal fear they showed every stranger in the region, he knew it was not that; he was fully aware that they feared him because he resembled Alijah Billington. Moreover, there was that disturbing suggestion made by the loafer, Seth, who called out to his companion, Luther, that 'he' had 'come back' with such evident seriousness that it was plain both of the old men had actually believed that Alijah Billington could and would come back to the country he had left to die a natural death in England over a century before.

He drove home almost unconscious of the brooding darkness of the hills upon hills, of the dusky valleys and the louring clouds, of the thin shining of the Miskatonic where light reflected from it under a rift in the middle-heaven; his thoughts were occupied with a thousand possibilities, a hundred avenues for research; and, in addition, he was curiously conscious of something further beneath and beyond the immediacy of his concerns—a growing conviction that he ought to abandon any further attempt to learn why it was that Alijah Billington was so feared, not alone by the ignorant and degenerate offspring of those Dunwich people of his own time, but by the white men, educated or not, among whom he had lived.

On the following day, Dewart was summoned to Boston by his cousin, Stephen Bates, to whom the final shipment of his belongings from England had been consigned; so for two days he was engaged in that city, arranging the transfer of those belongings to the house off the Aylesbury Pike beyond Arkham; and on the third, he occupied himself very largely in opening packing-cases and crates, and distributing his various possessions about his house. Among these final belongings was the set of directives which had been given him by his mother, and which had come down from Alijah Billington. As a result of his recent investigations, Dewart was now doubly anxious to re-examine this paper; so, having disposed of all the larger articles, he set about searching for it remembering that when his mother had given it to him, it was sealed in a large manila envelope, bearing her name in her father's hand.

After about an hour of rummaging through various documents, and what appeared to be a file of letters, he came upon the remembered manila envelope, and immediately broke the seal which his mother had put upon it after reading the instructions to him a fortnight before her death, which had taken place years ago. The paper, he decided, was not the original document penned by Alijah, but one that had been copied, probably by Laban in his old age, which would make the instructions he now held actually considerably less than a century old. Yet the signature was in Alijah's name, and Dewart doubted that Laban had altered or changed anything in any way.

Dewart carried a pot of coffee which he had been brewing into the study, and, sipping coffee, he laid the instructions out before him and began to read. The paper was undated, but the script, written in a firm, clear hand, was legible and easy to read.

'In regard to the American property in the Commonwealth of Massachusetts, I adjure all who come after me that this said property is better and wiser kept in the family for reasons it is better not to know. Though I consider it unlikely that anyone should set sail again for the American shore, if it so be, I adjure him who treads upon that property to observe certain rules, the sense of which shall be found within such books as have been left in the house known as Billington's house in the wood known as Billington's, the said rules being, to wit:

'He is not to cause the water to cease flowing about the island of the tower, nor to molest the tower in any way, nor to entreat of the stones.

'He is not to open the door which leads to strange time and place, nor to invite Him Who lurks at the threshold, nor to call out to the hills.

'He is not to disturb the frogs, particularly the bullfrogs of the marshland between the tower and the house, nor the fire-flies, nor the birds known as whippoor-wills, lest he abandon his locks and his guards.

'He is not to touch upon the window, seeking to change it in any way.

'He is not to sell or otherwise make disposition of the property without inserting a clause to hold that the island and the tower are in nowise disturbed, nor the window be alter'd except it be destroy'd.'

The signature, completely copied out, was 'Alijah Phineas Billington.'

In the light of what he had turned up, fragmentary as it was, this comparatively brief paper was of far more than passing interest. Dewart was at a considerable loss to account for his great-great-grandfather's concern about the tower—which must beyond question be the tower he had seen and investigated—about the bog or marshy area, and about the window—which, likewise, must be that window in the study.

Dewart looked up at it curiously. What was there about it that should demand such care? Certainly the pattern was interesting; it was one of concentric circles with rays travelling outward from the centre, and the multi-coloured glass which framed the round central piece made it especially bright now in late afternoon, when the sunlight hit it squarely. As he looked at it, he was conscious of an exceedingly curious reaction; the leaded circles seemed to move, to spin around; the rayed lines to tremble and writhe; and something like a depiction of a portrait or a scene seemed to begin forming among the panes. Dewart immediately closed his eyes tightly and shook his head; then he ventured a quick glance at the window. There was nothing whatever odd about it, save its being there. Yet the momentary impression had been so vivid that Dewart could not help but feel that he had either been working too hard and had had a dizzy spell, or had been drinking too much coffee—possibly a combination of both; for Dewart was one of those not unusual people who can begin on a pot of coffee and by slow stages consume it, preferably black, but with plenty of sugar.

He put the documents down, and removed the coffee-pot to the kitchen. Returning, he gazed at the leaded window once more. The study was now growing dim with twilight, for the sun was slipping behind the wall of trees to westward, and, as a result, the leaded window was illuminated by a fine blaze of golden and copper light. It was quite possible, reflected Dewart, that he had been tricked into fancying something by the ever-fluid light of the sun at this hour. He lowered his gaze and went calmly about his business, which consisted of returning the set of instructions to the manila envelope, and, having filed the envelope away, he went on about the arranging of the boxes and cases of letters and other papers which remained to be put away.

In this manner he passed the hour of twilight.

Having completed his somewhat tiresome task, he put out the lamp he had lit, and instead lit a small bracket lamp in the kitchen. He intended to go outside for a short walk, for the evening was mild and mellow, hazy with smoke from burning grass or brush somewhere near Arkham, and a waxing moon hung low in the west; but, in setting out, he walked the length of his house to go out the front door, and, happening to pass the study, his eye was caught by the leaded window.

What he saw there brought him to an immediate halt. By some trick or arrangement of moonlight on the leaded panes, the window gave the unmistakable appearance of a grotesquely malformed head. Dewart stared in fascination; he could discern eyes or pits of eyes, and what must certainly be a mouth of a kind, together with a vast dome-like forehead—but there semblance to anything human ceased, and the nebulous outline trailed off in a hideous representation of what seemed to be tentacles. This time blinking his eyes did Dewart no good whatever; the horrible grotesque was apparently fixed. First the sun, and now the moon, thought Dewart, and in a few moments reasoned that his great-great-grandfather had had the window designed for this purpose.

Nevertheless, this ready explanation did not satisfy him. He moved a chair over to the row of shelves beneath the window, mounted from the chair to the top of the stout book-casing, and so stood squarely before the window, his intention being to examine every pane so well as the whole. But he had hardly got into position to do so, when the entire window seemed to become animated, as if the moonlight had turned to witchfire, as if the outline, spectral as it was, had come to malign life.

As quickly as it had begun, the illusion ceased. He was left somewhat shaken, but sound, standing before the central circle of the window, which fortunately, appeared to be of clear glass, and there, looking in upon him was the moon, and between the glass and the moon, the eerie whiteness of the tower rising out of the ravine with the trees tall and dark all around, and the tower visible only through this opening, gleaming dully in the wan light of the moon. He stared outward. Surely his eyes were badly in need of attention, or did he see something flaffing darkly around the tower—not at the base, for that was not visible, but at the conical roof? Dewart shook his head; doubtless the moonlight, and perhaps vapors rising from the marsh beyond the house at this elevation made unfamiliar patterns.

Yet he was upset. He got down from the bookcase and walked over to the threshold of the study. He looked back. The window showed a faint glow—nothing more; even as he gazed at it, the glow faded perceptibly. This was consistent with the withdrawing light of the moon, and Dewart was conscious of feeling some relief. Admittedly, the mounting events of the evening had given him some reason to be upset, but he reasoned that his great-great-grandfather's inexplicable instructions had served to put him into the mood to misconstrue things heard and seen.

He went out for his walk, as he had planned; but,

because of the darkness which now fell with the vanishing of the moon, he did not strike off into the woods, but instead walked along the roadway which led down to the Aylesbury Pike. Such was his state of mind, however, that he constantly had the conviction that he was not alone, that he was being followed, and he looked furtively from time to time among the close pressing trees for sight of any animal, or the gleaming eyes which might betray the presence of an animal. But he saw nothing. Overhead the stars shone with increasing brightness, now that the moon had gone down.

He came out to the Aylesbury Pike. Strangely, the sight and sound of cars speeding along the highway was reassuring. He reflected that he was too much alone, and that some day soon he must ask his cousin, Stephen Bates, to come down and spend a fortnight with him. As he stood there, he was conscious of a faint orange glow on the horizon rising in the direction of Dunwich, and he thought he heard sounds that might have been voices raised in fright. He thought that perhaps one of the ramshackle old buildings in the Dunwich country had caught fire, and watched until the glow seemed to recede. Then he turned and went back the way he had come.

In the night he awoke, overpoweringly conscious of being watched, but with a sense of the benign about it. He slept restlessly, and when he woke, he woke very tired still, and restless, as if he had not slept at all, but had been on his feet much of the night. The clothes he had folded carefully over a chair were in disorder, though he could not remember having got up in the night and disarranging them.

Despite the lack of electricity in his home, Dewart had a small battery radio which he used sparingly— very rarely for a musical programme, but rather consistently for news-broadcasts, particularly a morning re-broadcast of news from the British Empire, which encouraged a dormant nostalgia, for it was regularly introduced by the strokes of Big Ben, which brought London back to him, London with all its yellow fogs, its ancient buildings, its quaint byways, and colourful passages. This re-broadcast was preceded by a flash of current national and state news from the Boston station, and this morning, when Dewart turned on the radio for his regular news from London, the state news was still coming over the air. He had cut in in the middle of a paragraph about a crime, evidently, and he listened casually and a little impatiently.

'. . . the time of the discovery of the body was an hour ago. No identification had been made up to the time we began broadcasting, but the body appears to be that of a countryman. No autopsy has yet been performed, but the body is so badly mangled and torn that it would seem as if the waves had beaten it up along rocks for a long time. However, since the body was found well up shore, beyond the line of the waves, and was not wet, the crime was apparently of land origin. The body has the appearance of having been thrown or dropped, as if from a passing aeroplane. One of the medical examiners has pointed out certain similarities to a series of crimes committed over a century ago in this region.'

This was apparently the final news item on the local broadcast, for immediately thereafter, an announcer prepared the way for the re-broadcast from London, which, no doubt, was in the form of a transcription out of New York. The news of this local crime, however, affected Dewart most singularly; he was not by nature prone to influence of this kind, though he had a secondary interest in criminological matters; but he had a most uneasy conviction amounting almost to foreboding that this crime was destined to have its imitations in the manner of the Jack the Ripper crimes in London or the Troppmann murders. He hardly listened to the re-broadcast from London; he was, in fact, busy reflecting that he had become far more sensitive to moods, to atmospheres, to events, since he had come to make his home in America; and he was curious to know by what means he had lost that former aloofness which had been so much a part of his existence in England.

He had meant, this morning, to look at his great-great-grandfather's instructions once more, and, breakfast over, he got out the manila envelope and set to work in an effort to wrest some meaning from what had been written. He turned specifically to the 'rules' or 'directives,' and began to ponder over them. He could not 'cause the water to cease flowing' because water had not flowed for some time around the tower island; as to molesting the tower, he supposed that by removing the inset stone he had already after a fashion molested it. But what under heaven did Alijah mean by adjuring him 'not to entreat of the stone'? What stones? Dewart could think of no other stones save those remnants which had reminded him of Stonehenge. If these were the stones to which Alijah referred, how then did he expect anyone to 'entreat of' them as if they had intelligence? He could not fathom it; perhaps Cousin Stephen Bates might know, if he remembered to show him when Bates came up.

He went on.

To what 'door' did his great-great-grandfather have reference? As a matter of fact, the whole adjuration was a complete puzzle. 'He is not to open the door which leads to strange time and place, nor to invite Him Who lurks at the threshold, nor to call out to the hills.' Could anything be more inexplicable! In a manner of speaking, this time, the present, would be strange to Alijah, thought Dewart. Could Alijah then have meant that he, being in his time, should not seek to learn anything of Alijah's time? That was a manifest possibility, but, if one accepted it, one must consider that Alijah must have meant something quite different by his 'strange place.' There was a sinister sound about that 'Him Who lurks at the threshold'; Dewart could not deny it—it had a sinister, ominous sound, and he thought quite soberly that it ought to be accompanied by a clash of cymbals and deep-throated rumbling of thunder. What threshold? And what *Him?* And finally, what in heaven's name did Alijah mean by adjuring his heir not 'to call out to the hills'? Dewart had a vision of himself or any other standing in the woods and calling out to the hills. It was not facetious imagination, but wore an aspect of the ludicrous. This, too, must be shown to Cousin Stephen.

He continued to the third adjuration. He had no desire and no inclination whatever to disturb the frogs, the fireflies, or the whippoorwills; so there was not likely to be any conflict with the instructions on that score. But—'lest he abandon his locks and guards'—great Heaven! was ever anything more frustrating, more inconclusive, more ambiguous? What locks? What guards? Clearly his great-great-grandfather wrote in riddles. Did he then wish his heir to seek the explanation of those riddles? And how, if so, was one to go about that? By disobeying the adjurations and waiting for something to happen? That did not seem either wise or efficient.

He put away the paper again, in mounting disgust. He had a growing sense of frustration; each and every way he turned, he encountered increasing knowledge and increasing bafflement; it was impossible to draw conclusions from which data as he had gathered, save that crusty old Alijah was manifestly engaged in some kind of activity which was not looked upon with favour by the natives. Secretly, Dewart thought that it was smuggling—probably up the Miskatonic and its tributary to the tower.

For the greater part of the day that remained, Dewart occupied himself with matters pertaining to the shipment he had unpacked on the previous day. There were forms to fill out, bills to be paid, and all the checking to be done. As he went down the list in his mother's hand, a list of her belongings into which he had never looked, he came upon an item marked 'Pkt. Bishop Lrs. to A. P. B.' The name 'Bishop' brought back to his immediate consciousness the old beldame he had interviewed in the Dunwich country. The packet was at hand, and he took it up. It was marked 'Bish'p Lrs.' in a hand not familiar to him, a crabbed script which was scarcely legible, and yet had about it a singular directness.

He opened the packet and there lay disclosed four letters of the fashion of many decades ago. They were not stamped, but rather marked with the fee paid, and had been sealed, for the broken seals still remained. The same crabbed hand which had marked the outside of the packet had also numbered the letters so that they were in sequence. Very carefully, Dewart opened the first of them; none in an envelope, but all were written on stout paper, and in very small script that was difficult to become accustomed to. He looked at each one briefly in turn, to establish the year; but none set it forth. Then he sat back to read them, taking them in order.

New Dunnich, 27 April

'Esteem'd Friend,

'Of matters concern'g which we have had certain converse, I have last night seen a Be'g which had ye appearance of such as we sought, with wings of dark substance and likewise as it were serpents running forth from Its body but attach'd to It. I call'd It to ye Hill, and contain'd It in ye circle, but onlie with ye greatest difficultie and hardship, so that 'twou'd but seem it is not likelie that ye circle is potent enough to contain such as These for long. I attempt'd converse with It, but did not well succeed, though from such as It did gibber, It came from Kadath in ye Cold Waste, which is nigh unto that Plateau of Leng mention'd in ye Booke. Divers Persons witness'd ye fire on ye Hill and spoke of it, and one among them is certain to make trouble, Wilbur Corey by name, he be'g of great opinion of himself and pry'g by nature. Woe to him shou'd he come to ye Hill when I am there, but I do not doubt, he will not come. I am eager and desirous of learn'g more of these matters of which ye Master was y^r honour'd grandsire, Rich'd B., whose Name shall ever be graven upon ye stones for Yogge-Sothothe and all ye Great Olde Ones. I rejoice you are once more within reach, and hope to call upon you so soon I may recover ye use of my Stallion, for I wou'd fain ride no other. I heard this day week in ye night time a great cry'g and scream'g from y^r Woode, and thought surelie you were back in ye House. I will shortlie call upon you if it suit y^r convenience, and meanwhile, Sir I am y^r true Servt.

Jonathan B.'

From the first, Dewart went on immediately to the second.

New Dunnich, 17 May.

'Honour'd Friend,

'Y^r note come to hand. I am griev'd my poor efforts have brought difficultie to you and to us and all those who serve Him Who Is Not To Be Named, or ye G. O. Ones altogether, but it came about in this way, that ye pry'g Fool, Wilbur Corey, did come upon me by surprise at ye stones as I was in ye midst of my Do'g, whereupon he cri'd out that I was a Warlock and wou'd suffer at his Word, at which I, becom'g mightilie disturb'd, turn'd upon him That with which I held converse, and he was much torn and bloodied and taken from my sight back whence That had come, to what bourne I know not, onlie that he will no more be seen in these parts in fit state to say whereof he saw and heard. I confesse I was sore affright'd by ye sight, and ye much more because I know not how Those Outside look upon us, and think often they are but pass'g grateful to us for afford'g them this open'g. Moreover, I fear overmuch what Others may linger Out There, ly'g in wait, for I have reason hav'g one even'g recentlie made some alterations in ye words as in ye Booke, and for a short space see'g Something trulie horrible in ye accustom'd place, a great Thing with a Shape that seem'd ever changing in a manner terrible to see, this Thing be'g accompani'd by lesser Be'gs which play'd upon instruments resembl'g flutes music most strange and unlike to any which I had ever before heard, see'g which and hear'g which, I desist'd in confusion and so caus'd ye said apparition to vanish all in good time. What this might have been I know not, nor is there any word in ye Book which wou'd set it forthe, unless it was some Daemon from Yr or beyond Nhhngr which lieth in far places on ye far side of Kadath in ye Cold Waste, and I entreate y^r opinion on this matter, and y^r advice, for I wou'd not that I be destroy'd in this quest ere it be finished. I hope I may see you not longe hence. I am, Sir, y^r obt. Serv't. by ye Sign of Kish.

Jonathan B.'

Evidently a considerable hiatus of time elapsed between this letter and the third, for, though the third was not marked by a date, the references to weather indicated the passage of at least a half year.

New Dun'ch.

'Honour'd Brother:—

'I am sore press'd to explain that which I came upon in ye snow last night, be'g great footprints, or better, I shou'd not say "footprints", for that they were not, be'g more like to ye prints of a claw of monstrous size, of diameter considerably more than a foot across, and of greater length, perhaps to that of two feet, and hav'g ye appearance of be'g webb'd or at least in part so, ye whole be'g most mysterious and strange. One such print was reported by Olney Bowen, who was off in ye woods a-hunting of turkeys, and, com'g back, spoke of it, none believ'g him save myself, and, not draw'g attention to myself, I listen'd and learn'd where it was ye track had been seen, thereafter go'g myself to witness it, and, see'g ye first of them, had sudden forebod'gs that others of ye like w'd be found deeper in ye woods; so mounted forthwith among ye trees and saw here and there such others, e'en as I had thought, and came upon a great number near ye stones, but had no sight of liv'g things of any nature whatsoever, but study'g ye prints, came to ye judgment that they were of *winged things,* for ye tracks did so lie as if they were made by creatures bear'g wings. I made ye circle around ye stones, and continu'd it in a wide manner, untill I came upon ye footprints of a lad, and these follow'd, e'en when I saw ye prints had increas'd in ye width between them, as if ye lad were runn'g, at which I was upset and alarm'd, and well I might be, for they end'd at ye edge of ye woode down ye far side of that Hill, and say ly'g in ye snow his gun, some feathers which had belong'd to a turkey, and a cap, by means of which I knew him for Jedediah Tyndal, a lad of fourteen summers, mak'g inquiry after whom this morn, discover'd him to be miss'g, as I had fear'd. After which judg'd that some Open'g had been left in some manner, and *Something* come through, but know not what It might have been, and entreat you if you know to point to whatever part of ye Booke it is I may find ye words to send It back, though it would seem from ye amount of ye prints I did see that there was more than one, and all of some size, and whether invisible or not I do not know for none hath had sight of them, myself be'g includ'd, and I w'd know especially whether these might be servts. of N. or of Yogge-Sothothe, or of Some Other, and if ye like hath e'er befall'n you. I entreat y^r haste in this matter lest these Be'gs ravage further, for they are apparentlie eaters of blood as are ye others, and none can say when they will again come forth from Outside and forage among us and hunt these people so they might have their food.

> Yogge-Sothothe Neblod Zin
> Jonathan B.'

The fourth letter was in some ways the most frightening. A kind of pall of astonished horror had been laid upon Dewart by the first three letters; but in the fourth there lay an incredible suggestion of shuddersome terror, though this was not so much evident in the words as in the implications.

'Honour'd Dear Friend:——

'As I was prepar'g for sleep last night I heard That which did come to my window and call out my Name and promis'd to come for me; but, be'g bold, I walk'd in ye darkness to that window and look'd out, at which, see'g noth'g, I did open ye window, and thereupon immediately smell'd such a charnel stench that it was almost o'erpower'g, and I fell back, whereupon Something com'g through ye window did touch my face as it were with ye substance of jellie, in part scal'd, and nauseous to ye touch, so that I nairlie took leave of my senses, and lay there for a time I do not know how long before I clos'd ye window again and went to my bed. But I had hardly gott into it ere ye house began to shake and discover'd it as because of ye Earth's shak'g as were Something walk'g upon it in ye neighbourhood, close by ye house, and once again I heard my Name call'd out and ye like promise made at which I made no answer whatsoever, but I thought onlie What have I done? that first ye winged creatures of N. came through ye opening left by ye misuse of ye words of ye Arab, and now this Be'g of which I had no knowledge unless he be that Walker on ye Wind who is known by severall Names, namely Windeego, Ithaka, or Loegar, which I have ne'er seen and may not see. I am much troubl'd in spirit lest it come to pass when I go and entreat of ye stones and call out to ye Hills it is not N. who comes nor C., but this other who roll'd my Name on his tongue in accents not of this Earth; and if this come to pass, I implore you to come in ye night and close ye portal lest there come others which ought not to walk with men for ye evill of ye Great Olde Ones is too great for such as we are if e'en ye Elder Gods have not destroy'd them but only imprison'd them in these spaces and depths to which ye stones reach in ye time of ye Stars and ye Moon. I believe I am in Mortall Peril, and w'd rejoice if it were not so, but I have heard my Name call'd in ye Night by no Thing of this Earth, and I fear greatly my time has come. I did not read y^r letter carefullie enough, and I misinterpreted y^r words for I misread when you wrote: "Doe not calle up Any that you cannot put downe; by ye which meane, Any that can in turn call up somewhat against you, whereby y^r powerfullest Devices may not avail. Ask allways of ye Lesser, lest ye Greater shall not desire to make Answer, and shall commande more than you." But if I have done wrong in this Cause, I implore you to bring ye remedy in time. Y^r Obt. Servt. in ye service of N.

Jonathan B.'

Dewart sat for a long time contemplating these letters. It was now clear to him that his great-great-grandfather had been engaged in some devilish matters, into which he had initiated Jonathan Bishop of Dunwich, but without adequately informing his protegé. The nature of the business escaped Dewart, for the time being, but it would seem now that it had to do with sorcery and necromancy. Yet the suggestions inherent in these letters were at one and the same time so terrible and so incredible, that he more than half believed they might be part of an elaborate hoax. There was one way of finding out, though a tedious one. The library of Miskatonic University in Arkham would still be open, and he could consult the files of the Arkham weeklies to discover, if possible the names of any persons who had disappeared or who had died strangely in the period between 1790 and 1815, which would certainly cover the time adequately enough.

He was loath to go; for one thing, there was still some checking to be done. For another, he did not look forward with relish to the task of again digging into the files of the paper, though the weeklies were small in size, with few pages, and it did not take long to examine them. So presently he set out, intending to work through the supper hour and into the evening, if it were possible for him to do so.

It was late when he finished his task.

He had found what he sought in the papers for the

year 1807, but he had found far more than he had sought. In tight-lipped horror, he had made a precise list of what he had discovered, and as soon as he reached the house in the woods, he sat down, trying to assimilate and analyse the facts he had uncovered.

There was, first, the disappearance of Wilbur Corey. Then followed the vanishing of the boy, Jedediah Tyndal. After that there were four or five other disappearances, with some distance among them, and finally, last of all, the vanishing of Jonathan Bishop himself! But Dewart's discoveries did not end with this series of vanishings. Even before Bishop disappeared, Corey and Tyndal had reappeared, one of them near New Plymouth, the other in the Kingsport country. Corey's body had been much torn and mangled, but Tyndal's bore scarcely a mark of any kind; both, however, were dead—*but not long dead*. Yet their remains had not been found until several months after their disappearance! In a hideously suggestive way, these findings lent substance to the Bishop letters. Yet, despite all this additional information, the pattern of events was far from clear, and the meaning as remote as ever.

Dewart thought increasingly of his cousin, Stephen Bates. Bates was a scholar, and an authority on early Massachusetts history. More than that, he had delved into many out-of-the-way corners, and it was possible that he might be of some help to Dewart. At the same time, some note of caution asserted itself within Dewart; he felt that he must walk carefully, he must take more time and carry on his investigation as solitarily as possible, without stirring any other person's curiosity. He was no sooner conscious of this conviction than he began to wonder why he entertained it; he thought that there was no reason why he should be so secretive, and yet, again, he had only begun to think so when he was back where he had been before, at a stubborn certainty that secrecy must be maintained, and he must have ever ready a plausible explanation of his interest in the past. This lay at hand in an antiquarian pleasure in architecture.

He filed his newspaper findings away with the packet of Bishop letters, and went to bed that night lost in deep, puzzled thought, ever seeking some explanation for those facts he had thus far uncovered, disjointed as they were.

Perhaps it was this concern with the things which had happened a century ago which caused him to dream that night. He had never had such dreams. He dreamed of great birds that fought and tore, birds with horribly distorted human aspects; he dreamed of monstrous beasts; and he dreamed of himself in strange roles. In his dreams he was an acolyte or priest. He garbed himself strangely and walked from the house into the Wood, around the marsh of the bull-frogs and the fireflies, to the stone tower. Lights shone, both in the tower and in the window of the study, flashing as if in signals. He came within the circle of Druidic stones and stood in the shadow of the tower and gazed up through the opening he had made, and, standing there, he called to the heavens in a hideous distortion of the Latin tongue. He recited a formula thrice and made designs on the sand, and suddenly, with a great rush, a being of horrible and repellent aspect appeared to flow through the opening from above into the tower and, filling it, flowed outward through the door, pushing Dewart aside and speaking to Dewart in a debased tongue demanding of him the sacrifice, whereupon Dewart ran fleetly to the circle of stones and directed the visitant to Dunwich, in which direction it then went, fluid as water, but of great and terrible aspect, squid-like or octopoid, passing among the trees as air, along the earth as water, of great and wonderful properties, which enabled it to seem partially or wholly invisible apparently at will. He dreamed that he stood listening there in the shadow of the tower, and soon there rose sweet to his ears the sound of screaming and crying in the night, after hearing which he waited yet a while until the thing came back bearing among its tentacles the sacrifice and departed whence it came, by way of the tower. All was then still, and he too returned the way he had come, and sought his bed.

In this way Dewart spent his night; and, as if his dreams exhausted him, in the morning he overslept; discovering which, when at last he woke, he leapt from bed, only to start backward and come down on his bed on his haunches, for his feet pained him. Since he was not given to trouble in his pedal extremities, he bent curiously to examine them, and discovered that his soles were much bruised and somewhat swollen, and his ankles torn and lacerated, as if by many brambles and briars. He was amazed, and yet he felt he should not be. Nevertheless, he was much puzzled as he tried to stand again, and found it somewhat easier, now that he expected a certain amount of discomfort; it was the initial shock of unexpected pain, rather than the degree of that pain, which had affected him so disagreeably.

With some difficulty he managed his socks and shoes, and once thus protected, he found that he was able to walk with a modicum of discomfort. But how had this come about? He reasoned at once that he must have been walking in his sleep. This was in itself somewhat surprising, for he had seldom before manifested any such tendency. Moreover, he must have walked from the house into the woods, to sustain the bruises and scratches which were so plain and so easy to identify. He began, slowly, to recall his dream; it did not come clearly, but he remembered that he was at the tower; so he finished dressing and went outside to discover, if possible, whether there was anywhere a trace of his having walked there.

He found none at first. It was not until he came to the tower itself that he saw in the pebbly sand near the circle of broken stones, the imprint of an unshod human foot which must surely be his. He followed this track, faint as it was, into the tower, and there, the better to see by, he struck a match.

By its feeble light, he saw something else.

He lit another and looked again, his thoughts chaotic with a sudden uprush of alarm and confusion. What he saw there was a splash against the foot of the stone steps, partly on the stair, partly on the sandy floor, a red, flaring splash which he knew before he put his finger gingerly to it was blood!

Dewart stood staring at it, unmindful of the naked footprints around him, unaware of the match burning down until the flame touched his fingers and he dropped it. He wanted to light yet another, but he could not bring himself to do it. He walked somewhat shakily out of the tower and stood leaning against the wall in the warm morning sunlight. He sought some order in his thoughts; clearly he had been delving too much into the past, and his imaginative faculties were being unhealthily stimulated. The tower, after all, had been open; it was possible for a rabbit or some other such animal to have taken refuge there, and a weasel to have come upon it and a battle to the death ensued; it was possible that an owl had flown down through the opening in the roof and captured a rat or some animal of similar proportions, though he must admit that the splash of blood seemed somewhat too large for such an explanation and, then, too, there was no supporting evidence, such as tufts of feathers, hair, or fur which would have been virtually unavoidable.

After a little while, he went resolutely back into the tower and lit another match. He looked for anything which would corroborate his theory. There was nothing. There was no evidence of a struggle which might have been explained as one of those common tragedies of nature. However, there was no evidence of anything more than that, either. It was simply a splash of what appeared to be blood in a place where there should be no such thing. Dewart tried to look at it calmly, without the instantaneous reference to that hideous dream of the night-time, which had erupted in his consciousness as a flower full-blown, the moment he had satisfied himself that it was blood in the tower. It was undeniable, but the splash was such a splash as might have been made by a dropping of blood from a little height, and something in passage. It made Dewart uneasy to admit this event to himself; because, having admitted it, he had no recourse but to admit also that he did not know how to explain either this or his dream, he could not account for a growing number of slight, but exceedingly strange incidents which had been occurring with increasing regularity.

He went outside again and walked away from the tower, back along the marsh past the wood, and to the house. He looked at his bed-clothing, and saw on the sheets the brown marks of blood from his ankles. He almost wished that he had gashed himself severely enough to account for the stain in the tower, but by no stretch of his imagination could he thus account for it. He changed the bedding, and then set about prosaically brewing himself a pot of coffee. He continued thoughtful, but especially so because he recognized for the first time that he was drawn now this way, now that, in diametrically opposite directions, as if there were two of him, or a split-personality crisis. It was high time, he thought, for Cousin Stephen Bates to come down—or anyone, to relieve the solitude if only temporarily. But he had no sooner come to this conclusion, when he found himself arguing against it with an extraordinary zest quite alien to his nature.

He persuaded himself finally to resume his checking, and carefully refrained from reading any further letter or document, lest his imagination be once again stimulated and he again suffer a night of dream-horror; and by mid-afternoon, he had recovered his normal *joie de vivre* to such an extent that he felt himself once more in routine. Resting, he turned on the radio for a programme of music, but instead, he got the news-cast. He listened half-heartedly. A French spokesman had outlined his concept of what ought to be done with the Saar, and a British statesman had issued a wonderfully ambiguous counter-statement. Rumours of starvation in Russia and China—these came with periodicity, he thought. The Governor of Massachusetts was ill. A telephone report from Arkham—he sat up to listen.

'We have been unable to obtain verification up to this time, but a disappearance has been reported from Arkham. A Dunwich resident reported that Jason Osborn, a middle-aged farmer residing in that section, disappeared during the night. A great deal of noise was heard by neighbours, according to the rumour, but no explanation has been offered. Mr. Osborn was not a wealthy man, he lived alone, and kidnapping is not thought to have been a motive.'

Coincidence shrieked in one corner of Ambrose Dewart's consciousness. But he was filled with such alarm, that he literally tore himself from the couch where he had lain down, and fell upon the radio to shut it off. Then, almost instinctively, he sat down and wrote a frantic letter to Stephen Bates, explaining that he needed Bates' company, and imploring him to come at no matter what cost. As soon as he had written it, he set out to mail it, but with each step he took, he felt a compulsion to retain the letter, to think again, to reconsider his position.

It took great physical and mental effort for him to drive into Arkham and deposit the letter to Stephen Bates beyond recall in the post-office of that city, whose ancient gambrel roofs and shuttered windows seemed to crouch and leer at him with ghastly camaraderie as he went by.

2

Manuscript by Stephen Bates

MOVED BY THE URGENCE OF THE SUMMONS FROM MY cousin, Ambrose Dewart, I arrived at the old Billington house within a week following my receipt of his letter. In the wake of my arrival, there took place a series of events which, starting from a most prosaic beginning, culminated in the circumstances which have caused me to set down this singular narrative to be added to those fragmentary data and various notes in Ambrose's hand.

I have said that the events began prosaically, but this is not precisely correct; I should say, rather, they were prosaic in juxtaposition to the later occurrences at and in the vicinity of the house in Billington's Wood. Episodic and unrelated as these events seemed to be, they were all in fact essential parts of one pattern, irrespective of time and space and place, as I was to discover. This was unfortunately anything but clear initially. But, from the beginning I found in my cousin some evidence of primary schizophrenia—or what I then thought to be schizophrenia, but later came to fear as something quite different and far more terrible.

This two-faceted aspect of Ambrose's personality made my own research far more difficult, for it took the avenues of friendly co-operation on the one hand, and sly, guarded hostility on the other. This was manifest from the beginning; the man who had written me that frantic note was a man who sincerely asked and needed some assistance towards an explanation of a problem in which he found himself caught, however inexplicably; but the man who met me in Arkham in response to my wire announcing my arrival was cool, cautious, and very much self-contained, making light of his need, and seeking from the very start of my visit to impose a limit of no more than a fortnight upon it—and preferably even less. He was courteous and even affable; but there was about him a curious reticence and an aloofness which were not in accord with the tone of the hasty scrawl he had sent to me.

'When I got your wire, I realized you didn't get my second letter,' he said in greeting me at the station in Arkham.

'If you sent one, I didn't get it.'

He shrugged and observed only that he had written to put my mind at ease in regard to his earlier letter. And from this beginning, he made the suggestion that he had resolved his difficulties without my assistance, though he was happy that I had come, even if the urgence of his letter were no longer a motivating factor.

Instinctively, as well as physically, I could not escape the impression that what he said was not quite true; I felt it was possible that he believed in what he was saying to me, but of this I could not be certain. I said only that I was happy to know that the pressing problem, at the instigation of which he had written to me, no longer seemed to him so imperative. This seemed to satisfy him, and he grew less uneasy, and more amenable, making a few small observations in regard to the nature of the country along the Aylesbury Pike, observations which surprised me because I had not thought him long enough in Massachusetts to have learned so much about the immediate and past history of the region in which he lived, a region which was not usual in that it was considerably more ancient than many other parts of the oldest inhabited areas of New England, a region which included strangely haunted Arkham, a mecca for scholars with architectural leanings, since its ancient gambrel roofs and fan-lighted doorways and ante-dated the less old but no less attractive Georgian and Greek revival houses along its shaded and shadowed streets; and which, on the other hand, included also such forgotten valleys of desolation, of degeneracy and decay as Dunwich, and only a little farther away, the accursed seaport town of Innsmouth —a country out of which has come many a half-whispered and suppressed rumour of murder, strange disappearances, curious cult-revivals, and many crimes and manifestations of degeneracy far worse, unmentionable in essence, and far more easily forgotten about than investigated for fear of what any investigation might uncover of matters far better hidden forever.

In this fashion we reached the house at last, and I found it as well preserved as it had been the last time I had seen it, some two decades before—indeed, as well preserved as it had always been, it seemed, as long as I could remember it, and my mother before me; a house which showed the ravages of time and of neglect far less than hundreds of other houses which had had far less of both years and desertion to contend with. In addition, Ambrose had restored it and re-furnished it a great deal, though nothing much but a new coat of paint had been given its front, which still stood out with a past century's dignity with its four tall square pillars built into its front elevation, and its squarely centred door, which set in a frame of singular architectural perfection. The interior in every way complemented the exterior; Ambrose's personal tastes had permitted no innovations out of character of the house, and the result, as I had expected it to be, was highly felicitous.

I observed everywhere the evidence of my cousin's preoccupation with matters he had barely mentioned to me in Boston some time ago—genealogical research, for the most part; this was particularly manifest in the yellowed papers seen in the study, and the ancient tomes which he had taken down from the laden shelves for consultation.

As we entered the study, I noticed the second of those curious facts which were later on to bulk so largely in my discoveries. I saw that Ambrose glanced involuntarily, and with a certain mixture of apprehension and expectation, at the leaded window set high in the wall of the study; when he looked away, I saw again that admixture of two opposites—both relief and disappointment. It was extraordinary almost to being uncanny. I said nothing, however, reasoning that at some point in the near future, however extended the cycle might be, whether of twenty-four hours or a week or more, Ambrose would reach again that stage at which he had been impelled originally to write me.

That time came sooner than I had expected.

We spent that evening in small talk, and I saw that Ambrose was very tired, since he suffered some obvious difficulty in keeping awake. Pleading tiredness myself, I relieved him by going to my own room, which he had shown me shortly after my arrival. However, I was far from tired; so I did not go to bed, but sat up for some time reading. Only after I had become somewhat indifferent to the novel I had brought along, did I put out my lamp—and this was sooner than I had expected to do so; for I found it extremely trying to become accustomed to my cousin's unfortunately necessary mode of lighting. The hour, I believed, looking back upon it now, must have been in the vicinity of midnight. I undressed in the darkness, which was not too dark, for the moonlight shone into one corner of the room and made a faint glowing which illumined all the room.

I had got but partially undressed when I was startled at the sound of a shout. I knew that my cousin and I were alone in the house; I knew that he expected no one else to join us. I realized instantly that, since I had not shouted, either it was my cousin who had, or it was not; and if it were not, then the shout was raised by an intruder. Without hesitation, I left my room and ran into the hall. I saw a white-robed figure descending the stairs, and hastened after it.

At this moment the shout came again, and I heard it distinctly—a strange, meaningless crying aloud. 'Iä!

Shub-Niggurath. Iä! Nyarlathotep!' And I recognized together, voice and shouter; it was my cousin Ambrose, and he was clearly walking in his sleep. I took him gently but firmly by the arm with the intention of guiding him back to his bed, but he resisted with unexpected vigour. I released him, and followed him; but when I saw that he meant to go out into the night, I again took hold of him and attempted to turn him. Once more he resisted, with very great strength, so great, in fact, that I was surprised he did not waken, for I opposed him, and finally after an almost exhausting time, I managed to turn him and guide him back up the stairs to his room, where he returned to his bed docilely enough.

I was both somewhat amused, and a little disturbed. I sat for a short while beside his bed, which was in the room used by the much-disliked Alijah, our great-great-grandfather, thinking he might awaken again. Since I sat in line with the window, I was able to look out, and did so from time to time, receiving the most curious impression that at irregular intervals a kind of glowing, as of a concealed light, shone from the conical roof of the old stone tower on the property and in line with this wall of the house. I was unable, however, to convince myself that this was not due to some property of the stones under the moonlight, though I watched the phenomenon for some time.

At length, however, I left my cousin's room. I was still wide awake; if anything, this little adventure of Ambrose's had awakened me still more. I left the door of my room open a little, corresponding to Ambrose's, and was thus prepared for any further rambling my cousin might do. He did not ramble, however; instead, he began to mutter and mumble in his uneasy sleep, and presently I found myself listening. Again, what he said made no sense to me. I was impelled to take down his words, and moved over into the moonlight to avoid lighting the lamp. Much of what he said was incoherent; not word of it could be distinguished, but there were occasional lucid sentences—lucid, that is, in the sense that they seemed to be sentences, however stilted and unnatural my cousin's voice sounded in his sleep. There were, in short, seven such sentences, and each occurred after an interval of perhaps five minutes of muttering and tossing, turning and mumbling. I took them down as well as I was able, making corrections later to bring their wording clear. In sequence, broken as I have said, by mutterings which were not intelligible, my cousin Ambrose murmured in his sleep these lines.

'To bring up Yogge-Sothothe thou shalt wait upon the sun in the fifth house, with Saturn in trine; then shault thou draw the pentagram of fire, saying the ninth verse thrice repeating which each Roodemas and Hallow's Eve causeth the Thing to breed in the Outside Spaces beyond the gate, of which Yogge-Sothothe is the Guardian.'

* * *

'He hath all knowledge; he knoweth where the Old Ones came through in the aeons past, and he knoweth where they will break through again.'

* * *

'Past, present, future—all are one in him.'

* * *

'The accused Billington did affirm that he caused no noises to be made, whereupon there ensued at once a great tittering and laughing, which fortunately for him was audible only to him.'

* * *

'Ah, ah!—the smell! *The smell! Aï! Aï! Nyarlatho-tep.*'

* * *

'That is not dead which can eternal lie, and with strange aeons even death may die.'

* * *

'In his house at R'lyeh—in his great house at R'lyeh —he lies not dead, but sleeping. . . .'

* * *

This extraordinary rigmarole was succeeded by a deep silence, out of which came soon the sound of my cousin's regular breathing, which told me that he had at last sunk into a quiet and natural sleep.

My first few hours at Billington's house were, therefore, filled with a variety of contradictory impressions. These were to continue. I had hardly put away the notes I had transcribed and got into bed and to sleep, still leaving my door open, and not closing Ambrose's, when I was startled awake, by the hurried banging of a door and the discovery of Ambrose looming up beside my bed, one hand and arm outreached as if to awaken me.

'Ambrose,' I cried. 'What is it?'

He was trembling, and his voice shook. 'Do you hear?' he asked shakily.

'Hear what?'

'Listen!'

I obeyed.

'What do you hear?'

'The wind in the trees.'

He gave a bitter laugh. ' "The wind gibbers with Their voices, and the earth mutters with Their consciousness." Wind, indeed! Is it only the wind?'

'Only the wind,' I replied firmly. 'Have you been having a nightmare, Ambrose?'

'No—no!' he answered in a cracked voice. 'Not to-night—it was just beginning, and then it stopped; something stopped it, and I was glad.'

I knew what had stopped it, and was gratified; but I said nothing.

He sat down on the bed, and put one hand affectionately on my shoulder. 'Stephen, I am glad you are here. But, if I should say things to you which should not seem in concord with that pleasure I feel, I beg you to disregard it. It seems sometimes I am not myself.'

'You've been working too hard.'

'Perhaps.' He raised his head, and now in the dim reflection of the moonlight, I saw how drawn his face was; he was listening again. 'No, no,' he said, 'it is not the wind in the trees, it is not even the winds among the stars, it is something farther away—something from Outside, Stephen. Can't you hear it?'

'I hear nothing,' I said gently, 'and perhaps if you could sleep you would hear nothing either.'

'Sleep does not matter,' he said enigmatically, speaking in a whisper, as if he feared some third person might hear. 'Sleep is worse.'

I got out of bed, walked over to the window, and threw it open. 'Come and listen, then,' I said.

He came over to my side and leaned against the windowframe.

'Wind in the trees—no more.'

He sighed. 'I will tell you tomorrow—if I can.'

'Tell me whenever you like. But why not now, when you feel like it?'

'Now?' He looked over his shoulder with dreadfully frightening implications. 'Now?' he repeated again, huskily. And then— 'What was it Alijah did at the tower? How did he entreat of the stones? What did he call out of the hills or the heavens?—I do not know which. And what was it lurked and at what threshold?' At the conclusion of this singular spate of baffling questions, he looked searchingly into my eyes in that half-darkness, and, shaking his head, said, 'You do not know. None does. But something is happening here, and before God I fear I have brought it about by some means I know not of.'

So saying, he turned abruptly and, with a curt 'Good night, Stephen,' he retired to his room and closed the door behind him.

I stood for a few moments, cold with amazement, at the open casement. Was it indeed but the wind whose voice came from the wood? Or was it something more? My cousin's bizarre performance left me shaken, ready to doubt my own senses. And suddenly, as I stood there, feeling the freshness of the wind against my body, I was conscious with a rapidly mounting oppression, with a crushing sense of despair, of a horrible

79

foulness, of a black, blasting evil of and around this woods-girt house, a cloying, infiltrating loathsomeness of the nethermost abysses of the human soul.

It was not purely imaginary; it was a tangible thing, for I was aware of the coolness of the air flowing in through the open window as *contrast*. The apprehension of evil, of terror and loathing, settled like a cloud in the room; I felt it pour from the walls like invisible fog. I walked away from the window and into the hall; it was the same out there. I went downstairs in the dark; nothing was changed—everywhere in this old house brooded a malign and terrible evil, and it was this, surely, which had affected my cousin. It required all my effort to cast off the oppression and despair I felt; it took conscious endeavour to repel the infiltration of terror which swept out from all the walls; it was a struggle against something invisible which had twice the force of a physical opponent; and, returning to my room, I realized that I was hesitant to sleep, lest in that sleep I become prey to that insidious penetration which sought to infect everything within reach as it had already infected this ancient house and its new habitant, my cousin Ambrose.

I remained therefore in a state of watchful sleep, drowsing a little, and resting. After perhaps an hour, the sense of brooding evil, of awful terror and loathsomeness receded and fell away as suddenly as it had come, but by this time I had achieved a state of reasonable comfort, and I did not make any attempt to fall into an even deeper sleep. I got up at dawn, dressed, and went downstairs. Ambrose was not yet down, and this afforded me a chance to examine some of the papers in the study.

These were of various kinds, though none was of a personal nature, such as letters to Ambrose. There were what appeared to be copies of newspaper accounts of curious happenings, particularly certain matters pertaining to Alijah Billington; there was a much annotated account of something which had taken place when America was young, to a protagonist put down as 'Richard Bellingham, or Bollinhan,' and identified, in my cousin's script, as 'R. Billington'; there were recent newspaper clippings concerning two disappearances in nearby Dunwich, of which I had read cursorily in the Boston newspapers prior to my coming to Arkham. I had no time to do more than glance at this extraordinary collection before I heard my cousin stirring, and left off to wait for him.

I had some purpose in waiting here, for I wished to observe Ambrose's reaction to the leaded window. As I half-expected he might, he gave it again an involuntary glance over one shoulder as he advanced into the room. I was not able, however, to determine whether this morning's Ambrose was the man who had met me in Arkham or that other, more recognizable cousin who had spoken to me in my room last night.

'I see you're up, Stephen. I'll get coffee and toast ready. There's a recent paper somewhere. I have to depend on rural delivery out of Arkham, you know—I don't get into town myself very much, and you couldn't pay a newsboy enough to cycle out this far—even if it weren't for. . . .'

He stopped abruptly. 'If it weren't for what?' I asked bluntly.

'For the reputation the house and the woods have.'

'Oh, yes.'

'You know about it?'

'I've heard some things.'

He stood for a moment and gazed at me, and I could see that he appeared to be caught in a dilemma, which suggested again that there was something he wished very much to tell me but feared to or, for some reason not yet manifest to me, was extremely reluctant to put into words. Then he turned and left the study.

I was interested neither in the recent newspaper—which was two days old—nor in the other documents and papers, for the time being; but turned instantly to the leaded window. For some reason, my cousin both feared this window and took pleasure in it—or rather, as I had seen, a *part* of him feared it, and something other in him enjoyed it. It was not unreasonable at all to suppose that that part of my cousin Ambrose which feared the window was one with that aspect of him I had seen in my room the previous night, and the other was akin to the drive which had impelled him in his sleep just prior to that scene in my room. I studied the window from several angles. The design, of course —which was of rayed concentric circles, with coloured panes, all in pastel shades save a few towards the central circle of apparently plain glass—was completely unique. Nothing like it existed, so far as I knew, in any of the stained glass windows of European cathedrals or American Gothics, neither in pattern, nor in colour-design, for the colours were unlike the stained glass windows of Europe and America in that they were singularly harmonious, seeming to flow or fuse into one another, despite being of various shades of blue, yellow, green and lavender, very light around the outer circle of panes, and very dark—almost black—near the central 'eye' of colourless glass. It was, in fact, as if the colour had been either washed out from the black central frame for the circle, or washed inward from the outer edge to make that darker portion, and the colours had been so well fused that any concentrated attention invariably tricked the eyes into believing that there might be some kind of movement of the colours themselves, as if they were still running and flowing together.

But this, manifestly, was not what had disturbed my cousin. Ambrose would certainly have reasoned this out for himself as quickly as I had done; nor would he be likely to be disturbed at the appearance of movement in the leaded circles, which was equally inevitable if one gazed at the window long enough, for the design was adroit and skilled, and it required a remarkable degree of technical ability as well as of imagination to have conceived and executed it. I was soon aware of these phenomena, which were capable of a scientific explanation, but, as I continued to gaze at this extraordinary window, I became uneasily aware of something more which did not yield quite so readily to rationalization. This was an occasional impression of a view or a portrait which appeared without any indication or warning in the window—not as if it were superimposed on it so much as *if it grew out of it*.

I realized instantly that this could not be a trick of light, for the window faced westward, and was at this hour in complete shadow, with all the house between it and the sun, nor was there, as I ascertained quickly enough by mounting the bookcase and looking out through the circle of colourless glass, anything at all within range of the window to reflect light upon it. I fixed my eyes upon the window with studied intent, but nothing came clear; I was unable to outline any complete picture, but that there was something suggestive about the window was inescapable, and I resolved to examine it closely under conditions more conducive towards bringing out anything which might lie concealed in the glass until such an hour as the light of sun or moon might be most favourable.

My cousin called from the kitchen that breakfast was ready, and I abandoned the window, knowing that I had ample time in which to complete any investigation I cared to make, since I had no intention of returning to Boston until I had learned what agitated Ambrose to so great a degree that, now I was here, he was unwilling or unable to confess it.

'I see you have been digging up some of the stories about Alijah Billington,' I said with designed directness, as I sat down at the table.

He nodded. 'You know my antiquarian and genealogical pursuits. Can you contribute anything?'

'Along the specific lines of your investigation?'

'Yes.'

I shook my head. 'I'm afraid not. It may be that

those papers might suggest something to me. Do you mind if I have a look at them?'

He hesitated. Clearly he did mind, but with equal clarity it was evident that he did not wish to deny me sight of what I had already seen, though he did not know how much I had read.

'Oh, you may look at them for all I care,' he said carelessly. 'I can't make very much out of them.' He swallowed some coffee, eyeing me thoughtfully. 'As a matter of fact, Stephen, I've got wound up in this business and I can't make head or tail out of it—and yet I have the strongest feeling that without knowing it, there are strange and terrible things happenings here —things that might be prevented, if one knew how.'

'What things?'

'I don't know.'

'You're speaking in riddles, Ambrose.'

'Yes!' he almost shouted. 'It is all a riddle. It is a complex of riddles, and I can find neither the beginning nor the end. I thought it began with Alijah—but I no longer think so. And how it will end I don't know.'

'That's why you sent for me?' I was delighted to see opposite me the cousin who had spoken to me in my room during the night.

He nodded.

'Then I had better know everything you have done.'

He forgot his breakfast and began to talk. It came out in a rush—everything that had happened since his arrival; he told me nothing whatsoever of his suspicions, and said so; these had no place in a narrative purely of events. He summarized or outlined the papers he had found—Laban's day-book, the newspaper accounts of Alijah's difficulties with the people of Arkham a hundred years and more ago, the Rev. Ward Phillips' writings, and so on; but these must be read, he said, before I could arrive at everything which he had come upon. It was indeed, as he had characterized it, a riddle, but, like him, I too felt that he had happened upon portions of a gigantic puzzle, and each piece fitted into it, no matter how unconnected they might seem to be. And, with each additional fact he told me, I became aware of the damnable suggestiveness of the trap in which my cousin Ambrose appeared to be caught. I made some attempt to calm him, and persuaded him to eat his breakfast, and to cease occupying all his waking and his sleeping hours with it, lest it become an uncontrollable obsession.

And immediately after breakfast, I set myself the task of dutifully reading everything Ambrose had found or taken down, in the order in which he himself had come upon these matters. It took me well over an hour to read the various papers and documents Ambrose laid out for me, and some little time beyond that to assimilate what I had read. It was indeed a 'complex of riddles,' as Ambrose had put it, but it was possible to draw certain general conclusions from the curious, apparently scattered facts presented in the writings and the notes.

The one primary fact which could not be escaped was that Alijah Billington (and Richard Billington before him?—Or should it be said, Richard Billington, and Alijah after him?) had been engaged in some kind of secret business the nature of which could not be determined from the available evidence. The possibility was that it was something evil, but in admitting this, it became necessary to take into account the superstition of provincial witnesses, the calumny of gossip, and the repetition of hearsay and legend which exaggerated out of all proportion to truth some trivial event. Common talk and legend indicated that Alijah Billington was disliked and feared, very largely because speculation about 'noises' heard in his woods at night was not satisfied. On the other hand, the Rev. Ward Phillips, the reviewer, John Druven, and presumably also the third of that trio who had paid a call on Alijah Billington—Deliverance Westripp, were not provincials. At least two of these gentlemen certainly believed that the business in which Alijah Billington was engaged was evil in nature.

But what was the evidence against Alijah to support such a contention? It was entirely circumstantial, in so far as the opposing gentlemen were concerned. It could be summed up very shortly.—There were inexplicable 'noises' resembling 'cries' or 'screams' of 'some animal' in the woods around Billington's house. Billington's chief critic, John Druven, disappeared under circumstances resembling other disappearances in the vicinity, and his body reappeared under similar circumstances. That is, there had been various disappearances, with recovery of the bodies of the missing persons a considerable time thereafter, all indicating that death had taken place shortly before discovery of the body. No explanation was ever offered to account for the weeks or months between disappearance and reappearance. Druven had left a damning note suggesting that Alijah had 'put something' into the food he had offered the three men who had called on him, not alone to impair their memories, but to summon Druven back to him or at least, render him incapable of disobeying the summons, should it come. This, of course, suggested that the trio *did* see something. But it was not evidence—not, that is, legally admissible evidence.

So much for the known case against Alijah Billington in his own time. However, a correlation of facts, suggestions, and hints, past and present, presented a picture considerably at variance with the portrait of Alijah Billington's ardent protestations and somewhat insolent defiance as to his innocence of the imputations made by Druven and others. Even without the affording of anything in the nature of a definite clue to the concerns of Alijah, the implications of the overall facts were startling, not to say frightening. These aspects, correlated without regard to the time period between the earliest of them and the most recent, made for a certain not easily shaken uneasiness, and a growing queasiness of doubt and uncertainty, for the underlying suggestions were hideous.

The first of these facts was Alijah Billington's own words, when he wrote to assail John Druven's review of the Rev. Ward Phillips' book, *Thaumaturgical Prodigies in the New-English Canaan*: '. . . there are things in existence better left alone and kept from the common speach.' Presumably Alijah Billington knew whereof he wrote, as the Rev. Ward Phillips retorted. If so, then the occasional entries in the boy, Laban's, journal or daybook took on an added significance. From this daybook it was possible to accept the fact that something had indeed been going on in the woods, with the aid of Alijah Billington. It was not conceivable, as my cousin Ambrose had thought, that it was smuggling; for it would have been sheer idiocy to accompany smuggling with 'noises' of the kind described in both the Arkham papers and also in the lad's daybook. No, it was something far more incredible, and there was a frighteningly suggestive parallel between one of the boy's entries and something within my own experience during the past twenty-four hours. The boy had written that he had found his Indian companion, Quamis, on his knees 'saying in a loud voice words in his language which I could not understand . . . but that had the sound of *Narlato* or *Narlotep*.' In the course of the previous night I had been roused by my cousin's somnambulistic voice shouting, 'Iä! Nyarlathotep.' That these words were one and the same, I could not doubt.

There was, then, a suggestion of worship in the Indian's attitude, but it remained to be admitted that the aborigines tended to worship anything which was not immediately understandable to them; this had been equally true of the American Indian as of the African Negro who had in many places set up the phonograph as an object of worship because it was completely beyond his comprehension.

One further question occurred to me from the daybook. It seemed to me that the missing pages roughly corresponded to the period during which the investigating trio had called upon Alijah Billington. If so, had the boy seen and recorded something which might aid in discovering what had actually taken place? And had his father then subsequently discovered what he had written and summarily destroyed it? Presumably, however, Alijah would have destroyed the entire book. If he were indeed engaged in some nefarious practices in the woods, what his son had written was damning. Yet the most effective passages had occurred after the missing pages. Perhaps Alijah had destroyed the offending pages, deeming that what the boy had previously written could not by any chance be admissible as evidence, and given the book back to him, perhaps abjuring him to write no more of such matters. That seemed to me the most likely explanation and would account in full for the fact that the book had remained to be found by my cousin Ambrose, because the most telling portions would then not have been written until after his father had torn out the pages he did not like.

However, the most disturbing of those correlated facts lay in the quotation from the curious document entitled, *Of Evill Sorceries done in New England of Daemons in no Humane Shape:* ' 'Tis said, one Richard *Billington,* being instructed partly by Evill Books, and partly by an antient Wonder-Worker amongst the Indian Savages . . . set up in the woods a great Ring of Stones inside which he say'd Prayers to the Divell, Place of Dragon, Namely, and sung certain Rites of Magick abominable by Scripture. . . . He privately shew'd great Fear about some Thing he had call'd out of the Sky at Night. There were in that year seven slayings in the woods near to *Richard Billington's* Stones. . . .' This passage was horribly suggestive, for two inescapable reasons. Richard Billington's time was almost two centuries ago. But, time nothwithstanding, there were parallel events between that time and Alijah Billington's, and again between Alijah Billington's and the present. There had been a 'circle of Stones' in Alijah's time; and there had been mysterious slayings likewise. There was now still what was left of a circle of stones, and there were once again beginning what seemed to be a series of slayings. It did not seem to me that, even making every possible allowance for chance and circumstances, these parallels could be coincidence.

But, denying coincidence, what then?

There was Alijah Billington's set of instructions, which adjured Ambrose Dewart and any other heir not 'to call out to the hills.' To draw the parallel, there was that 'Thing he had call'd out of the Sky at Night' so feared by Richard Billington. If coincidence were to be ruled out, there was this left. And this was even far more improbable than coincidence. But there was a key; however incomprehensible were the instructions Alijah had left, he had pointed out that 'the sense' of those rules 'shall be found within such books as have been left in the house known as Billington's house in the woods known as Billington'—in short, here, within these walls, presumably within this study.

The problem levied straining demands upon my credulity. Accepting the fact that Alijah Billington had been engaged in something he wished no one but the Indian, Quamis, to know about, it was possible to concede that somehow he had made away with John Druven. His practices then, must have been illegal; moreover, the precise manner of Druven's death was something to arouse much conjecture not only about Alijah but about the methods he had used to encompass Druven's end in a fashion similar to the slayings in the Dunwich country. The progression was a logical one from the acceptance of the fundamental premise that Alijah had managed to do away with Druven, to the secondary premise that he had also had a hand in the other slayings. The pattern was the same.

But along this path there lay a succession of admissions and conjectures which required so major a concession to accept that anyone hoping to cope with them would shortly find himself completely at sea, unless he cast off everything he had previously believed and started afresh. If Richard Billington did indeed call some 'Thing' out of the sky at night, what was it? No such 'Thing' was known to science, unless it might conceivably be accepted tentatively that something related to the now extinct pterodactyl had still existed two centuries ago. But this seemed even less probable than the other explanation; science had already definitely settled the matter of the pterodactyl; science had recorded nothing of any other flying 'Thing.' But then, none had anywhere written that the 'Thing' had flown. How then had it come out of the sky if it had not flown?

I shook my head in increasing bewilderment, and my cousin, coming in, smiled somewhat tensely.

'Is it too much for you, too, Stephen?'

'If I think overmuch about it, yes. But the instructions Alijah left indicate that the key lies in the books on these shelves. Have you looked at them?'

'What books, then, Stephen? There is no single clue.'

'On the contrary, I disagree with you. We have several. Nyarlathotep or Narlatop or whichever way you spell it. Yog-Sotot or Yogge-Sothothe—again, as you like to spell it. These have recurred in Laban's journal, in Mrs. Bishop's rambling account, in the letters from Jonathan Bishop—and there are certain other references in the Bishop letters which we might try to find in these old books.'

I turned once more to the Bishop letters, to which Ambrose had attached his findings from the files of the Arkham papers concerning the deaths of those persons of whom Jonathan Bishop had written. There was a disturbing parallel in these, too, which I had not the heart to mention to Ambrose, since he looked unwell and ravaged as by lack of sleep; but it could not be escaped that even as meddlesome persons who had spied upon Jonathan Bishop disappeared and were subsequently found later on, so it had happened to John Druven, who meddled incontinently in the business of Alijah Billington. Moreover, whatever one might think about the improbability of events, it was undeniable that the persons of whom Jonathan Bishop had written had indeed vanished, for the accounts were in the papers for all who wished to read.

'Even so,' said my cousin Ambrose when I looked up again, 'I would not know where to begin. All these books are old, and many of them are difficult to read. Some of them, I think, are bound manuscripts.'

'Never mind. There is plenty of time. We need not do it today.'

He seemed relieved at this and was about to carry forward the conversation when a knock sounded on the great outer door, and he rose to answer it. Listening, I heard him admit someone, and hastily put the papers and documents I had been reading out of sight. But he did not bring his visitors, for there were two, into the study, and, after half an hour, he let them out again and returned to the room.

'That was two of the county officials,' he explained. 'They are looking into the deaths which have occurred —the disappearances, rather—near Dunwich. That is an awful thing, I understand; if they are all to be found as the first one was, it will be something none in these parts will be likely to forget.'

I pointed out that Dunwich was notoriously decadent. 'But what was it they came to see you about, Ambrose?'

'It seems there are reports of noises—screams, he said—heard by some of the residents, and, since we are not too far from that region from which Osborn vanished, he thought I might have heard something.'

'But, of course, you didn't.'

'No, certainly not.'

The sinister similarities of the patterns of past and present did not seem to occur to him, or, if they did so, he gave no sign of it. I did not see fit to draw his attention to them, and changed the subject. I told him I had put the papers away, and suggested that we take a walk before luncheon, maintaining that the fresh air would do him good. To this he assented readily enough.

Accordingly, we set out. A brisk wind had sprung up, filled with intimations that the winter season was not far away; leaves fell in some quantity from the ancient trees, looking at which I was reminded uneasily of the reverence in which the ancient Druids had held trees. But this was a passing impression undoubtedly brought about by my preoccupation with the circle of stones in the vicinity of the round tower—for my proposed 'walk' was nothing more or less than a round-about way of getting myself to the tower in my cousin's company, lest he think that I desired to visit it, as certainly I would ultimately have done, alone, had I not done so in his company.

Rather deliberately, I chose a circuitous way, avoiding the marshy area which lay between the tower and the house, and going around to come upon the tower from the south, along the dried-up bed of that one-time tributary of the Miskatonic. My cousin commented from time to time upon the ancientness of the trees, and repeatedly observed that there was nowhere even so much as a stump which bore the mark of an axe or saw; I could not determine whether the note in his voice was one of pride or of dubiety. I mentioned that the old oaks were akin to Druid's trees, and he looked sharply at me. What did I know of Druids? he wanted to know. I replied that I knew comparatively little. Did I ever think that there might be some basic connection among many ancient religions or religious beliefs, such as the Druidic? It had not occurred to me, and I said so. Myth-patterns, of course, were fundamentally similar; all grew out of a fear of or curiosity about the unknown, and the mythmakers we had always with us; but one must differentiate between mere myth-patterns and religious beliefs, as between superstitions and legends on the one hand and credos and principles of ethics and morals on the other. To all this he said nothing.

We walked for some time in silence, and then a most curious incident took place. It happened just as we came to the dried-up bed of that tributary.

'Ah,' he said in a rather coarse voice unlike his natural tones, 'here we are at the Misquamacus.'

'The what?' I asked, looking at him in what must have been astonishment.

He looked at me in return, and his eyes seemed visibly to refocus. He stammered. 'W-what? W-w-what was that, Stephen?'

'What did you say the name of this stream was?'

He shook his head. 'I have no idea.'

'But you just named it.'

'Why, that is impossible. I don't know that it ever had a name.'

He seemed genuinely surprised, and a little angry. Seeing this, I did not press the point; I said that perhaps I had not heard rightly, or perhaps my imagination had begun to play pranks on me; but he had just the same given a name to the one-time stream which had flowed there. And the name he had given it sounded in every particular like the name of that 'antient Wonder-Worker' among the Wampanaugs, that old 'Wizard' who had supposedly at last vanquished and locked away the 'Thing' which had plagued Richard Billington!

The incident affected me very unpleasantly. I had already had some hint that the difficulty in which my cousin was involved was of far graver nature than he, or I for that matter, had apprehended. The nature of this apparently casual revelation increased that apprehension towards conviction. But I was shortly to experience even more striking confirmation of my suspicions.

Without any further passage of words between us, we made our way with ease up the dried bed of that tributary and presently broke out of the surrounding underbrush to the place of the tower, an island of gravel and sand, save for the rocks which jutted out around the tower in a crude circle. My cousin had spoken of these stones as 'Druidic,' but this I saw at a glance they did not seem to be, for these had none of the appearance of design so manifest in the Stonehenge survivals, for instance. Yet this circle of stones, now much broken, or encompassed by the accretion of years, some of it oddly barren alluvial deposit, bore the unmistakable signs of having been the handiwork of man; it had the aspect of purpose, rather than of design, and looked as if it might have been intended solely as a frame for the round tower, which, upon examination, I found all that I had been led to expect it would be in the light of the notes and documents I had read.

Now, I had seen and scrutinized this tower quite often before, but I had no sooner entered within the circle of broken stones than it was as if this were indeed my initial visit to the site. This I laid in part to my illuminating reading of the data Ambrose had put together; but in part it was caused also by a certain change in atmosphere. I was conscious of this at once; whereas heretofore the tower had impressed me as a forlorn old relic of an age lost in the dim past, I now had the instant conviction that it was something which was quite apart from time. Possibly this arose from the very knowledge of its age which had previously given rise to its aura of age, but quite possibly it did not, for the stone tower, which had often seemed a sunlit reminder of ages past, seemed now a squat, almost fearsome structure which had about it an aura of malign imperviousness to time, and accompanied by the faint suggestion of a disturbingly charnel odour.

Nevertheless, I advanced upon it as if it were new—and indeed, it required no imagination to believe that it was a new experience for me. I knew the aspect of the stones very well, but I wished to stand within and examine the carvings along the stone stair, as well as that figure or design cut into the large, newer stone which my cousin had dislodged from the roof. It was immediately apparent that the design carved along the stairs was in miniature the precise design of the leaded window in the study of my cousin's house. On the other hand, the design on the dislodged stone was curiously antipodal—a star as opposed to a circle, a lozenge and a pillar of flame or some such representation, as opposed to rayed lines. I was about to remark on the similarity of the repetitive design, when my cousin appeared in the doorway and something in his voice warned me to be still.

'Have you found anything?'

It was not only indifference in his voice; it was hostility. I divined instantly that my cousin was once more the man who had met me at the station in Arkham and had so manifestly wished me back in Boston. I could not avoid the question which immediately came to mind—to what degree had his proximity to the tower influenced his mood? But I said nothing, neither of what I thought, nor of what I had discovered; I observed only that the tower seemed to be very old and the designs very primitive, but 'without meaning'; and, though his eyes brooded upon me for a few moments, darkly and sombrely, he seemed to be satisfied, and retired from the threshold saying gruffly that it was time we returned to the house, it would soon be luncheon time, and he did not want to be too long in preparing it.

I responded to his mood, and came along quite readily, chatting cheerfully on the subject of his culinary talents, suggesting all the while that he should obtain the services of a good cook and relieve himself of a task which, however pleasant as a diversion, must inevitably become depressingly tiresome, and ultimately, as we came within sight of the house, urging that we forego lunch and make a trip into Arkham to have lunch instead at one of the restaurants there.

To this he assented agreeably enough, though I had not thought he would, and in a short time we were driving along the Aylesbury Pike in the direction of that ancient, haunted town, where I now hoped for some opportunity to leave my cousin long enough to have a look in at the library of Miskatonic University and discover for myself, if possible, to what degree of truth my cousin's notes had followed the accounts of Alijah Billington's activities in the columns of the Arkham newspapers.

That opportunity came sooner than I expected, for we had hardly finished lunch before Ambrose remembered several errands that he ought to do. He invited me to accompany him, but I declined, saying that I wished to stop in at the library and pay my respects to Dr. Armitage Harper, whom I had met a year ago at a scientific gathering in Boston, and, ascertaining that Ambrose would be gone for an hour, arranged to meet him at the College Street entrance to the Quadrangle at the expiration of that time.

Dr. Harper, who had retired from more active duty, had an office to himself on the second floor of the building which housed the Miskatonic Library, and was there available to bibliophiles and fellow-experts in Massachusetts history, on which he was an authority. He was a distinguished old gentleman, by no means betraying his seventy-odd years in the trim cut of his iron-grey moustache and Van Dyke and the alertness of his dark eyes. Despite having spoken to me on but two occasions, the last of which was almost a year ago, he recognized me after but a momentary hesitation, and seemed quite pleased to see me, explaining that he had been investigating a book by a Middle-Westerner whose work had been recommended to him, but that he found it diffuse, if fascinating. 'A far cry from Thoreau,' he said, smiling genially, and permitting me to see that the book he now laid aside was Sherwood Anderson's *Winesburg, Ohio*.

'What brings you to Arkham, Mr. Bates?' he asked, leaning back in his chair.

I replied that I was visiting my cousin, Ambrose Dewart, but, since I saw that the name meant nothing

96

to him, I added the explanation that my cousin was the heir of the Billington property, and that it was in connection with my visit there that I had now taken the liberty of consulting him.

'Billington is an old name in this area of Massachusetts,' said Dr. Harper dryly.

I answered that I had gathered as much, but that none seemed willing to say what kind of an old name, and, as far as I could ascertain, it was certainly not one held up to lasting respect.

'Armigerous, I believe,' he said. 'I have the coat of arms somewhere in the files here.'

Undoubtedly armigerous, I knew. But what in plain fact could Dr. Harper tell me of Richard Billington or, for that matter, of Alijah Billington?

The old man smiled, his eyes crinkling. 'We have some references to Richard in certain books—not very complimentary, I fear; and all that is known of Alijah appears to be chronicled in the files of the weekly papers of his own day.'

This was unsatisfactory, and my expression must have told him so.

'But you will know that,' he continued.

I agreed that I knew what was in print. I added that I had been impressed by the similarity between the accounts pertaining to Richard Billington and those referring to Alijah. Both, it would appear, had been engaged in practices which, if not proved illegal, were yet highly suspect.

Dr. Harper grew grave. He was silent for a few moments with that silence which indicates a struggle within, as to whether to speak or not. But presently he began to speak, with the air of measuring what he said. Yes, he had known of the legends about the Billingtons and about Billington's Wood for many years; they were, in fact, a rather essential part of Massachusetts lore—something almost in the nature of a hold-over from the days of the witchcraft excitement, though, in point of chronology, some of the stories antedated the time of the trials. There was apparently some basis for the legends in actual circumstances, though it was impossible to tell from this perspective what degree of truth served to lend credence to the grotesque legends handed down many years ago, and at one time easily believed, however much they were forgotten now. It was, however, a fact that Richard Billington was at one time looked upon as a wizard or warlock, and that Alijah Billington had earned for himself the reputation of doing dark deeds in his woods at night. One must expect that stories could not be prevented from accumulating on bases like these; such stories had promptly made their appearance and, in making the rounds, had subsequently added a great many facets which soon lifted the original stories out of the realms of the strange and fearsome into that of grotesque and incredible. In such fashion the original grain of truth was anything but manifest.

It did seem fairly certain, however, he admitted, that both the Billingtons were up to 'something.' Looking back upon it now, a century and more away from it, the practices of the Billingtons may or may not have been related to witchcraft; they may also or may not have been related to certain other rites, of which he, Harper, had had intimations from time to time, rites common in the backwoods country, the Dunwich and Innsmouth regions, for instance, rites which belonged properly, by their nature, to an ancient and alien race, for nothing in them suggested anything which could be said to have had its origin with man—unless one were to except some of the Druidic rites, in which worship of invisible beings in trees and the like was a commonplace.

Did he mean to imply that the Billingtons had worshipped dryads or some such similar mythological figure? I asked.

No, he did not have dryads in mind. There were certain strange and horrible survivals of religions or cults far more ancient than anything known to man.

These were so minor, comparatively speaking, that scientists and other investigators usually failed to disturb them, with the result that it was left to lesser scholars to document as much as was possible to know of the ancient religions and beliefs of the more primitive peoples of the earth.

In his opinion, then, my ancestors practised some strange, primitive type of religion?

In a manner of speaking, yes. He added that there was quite obviously—if I had read the records—a very strong possibility that the religious rites practised by Richard and Alijah Billington involved human sacrifice, but nothing had ever been proved. Yet both Richard and Alijah disappeared—Richard no one knew where, Alijah to England, where he had died. All legends and old wives' tales of Richard's survival were nonsense, he affirmed; such tales rose too easily, and were disseminated by the credulous. Richard survived and Alijah survived only in so far as the line was carried on in Ambrose Dewart, and, for that matter, myself; contrary accounts had their origin in such scriveners who sought to shock and dismay the reading public by greatly-coloured accounts of trivial incidents which had set flame to their imagination. However, he conceded, there was another type of survival—something known as psychic residue, the lingering of evil in places where evil had flourished.

'Or of good?' I asked.

'Let us just say of "force," ' he replied, smiling again. 'It is quite possible that force or violence of some kind lingers at Billington's house. Come, Mr. Bates—perhaps you yourself have felt it.'

'I have.'

He was astonished, and not agreeably so. He started a little, and then once more essayed a short smile. 'In that case, I need tell you nothing about it.'

'On the contrary, go ahead and let me at least hear your explanation of it. I have felt an all-consuming evil in that old house, and I do not know what to make of it.'

'Then it would seem that evil had been done there—perhaps the evil which became the primary basis for the stories later told of Richard and Alijah Billington. Of what nature, Mr. Bates?'

I could not easily explain, for putting my experience into words removed the fear and horror from it—reactions I had not at first known, but which came back in retrospect. Yet Dr. Harper listened gravely and did not interrupt, and, at the end of my brief account, he sat for a few moments in brooding thought.

'And how does Mr. Dewart react to all this?' he asked finally.

'That, more than anything else, is what brings me here.' Thereupon I launched into a somewhat guarded account of the apparent dual personality of my cousin, omitting as many details as I could, so that I might not keep Ambrose waiting.

Dr. Harper listened with close attention, and when I had finished he sat again in contemplative silence before he ventured the opinion that, manifestly, the house and the wood had a 'bad effect' on my cousin. It might indeed be well if he were to be removed from the house for a while—'Let us say, for the winter.'—so that the effect of such removal might be gauged on him. Where could he go?

I said promptly that he might come to my home in Boston, but admitted that I had hoped to take the opportunity to study among some of the ancient books in the library of my cousin's house—the Billington books. With my cousin's consent, these might well be taken along. But I doubted very much that Ambrose would agree to spend the winter in Boston, unless I caught him in the proper mood, and I said as much to Dr. Harper, who countered immediately with the strongest urging that Ambrose be convinced that it would be for his own good to change his residence for a short time, particularly in view of the Dunwich events, which boded no good for the vicinity and its residents.

I bade Dr. Harper farewell and went outside to stand in the autumn sunlight waiting for Ambrose, who came shortly past the hour. He was morose and moody, as I could plainly see, and made no conversational opening for some distance out of the city, and then only asked curtly whether I had seen Dr. Harper. He did not ask me to elaborate on my admission that I had, nor would I have done so, for he would have been offended if he had thought that we had discussed him in any way —offended, and perhaps something more than that. Thus we drove all the way back to the house in silence.

It was now late afternoon, and my cousin immediately set about getting the evening meal, while I busied myself in the library. I did not know where to begin to make the selections from among the books for those I hoped to persuade Ambrose to let me take along with him, but I looked into one after another, in search of any mention whatever of those key words which had been repeated in the persons and documents to such a consistent degree that they might be said to afford clues to the problem my cousin faced. Many of the books on the shelves proved to be chronicles of some historical and genealogical value concerning the region and its families; but in the main these appeared to be the orthodox accounts, doubtless subsidized by individuals, family groups, or organizations of some kind, and offered nothing of interest to anyone save the student of genealogy, filled as they were with quaint illustrations of family trees. Among these books, however, were others, which were not at all orthodox, some very worn, some of leather smoothed by wear decades ago. Of these a very few were in languages foreign to me, a few others in Latin, and some in English black-letter, while four of them were manuscript transcriptions—apparently incomplete—though bound. It was among this latter group that I hoped to find what I sought.

I thought at first that either Richard or Alijah Billington had made the laborious transcriptions, but only a little examination was enough to inform me that such was not the case, for the spelling was often too crude for it to be that of persons of education, such as both Billingtons were, to the best of my knowledge. Moreover, there were annotations made in a later hand, which was almost certainly that of Alijah Billington. There was nothing to show that any of the manuscript books had ever belonged to Richard Billington, but they might have been his property, for most of them were quite old, and, while no date appeared anywhere in the script, it seemed very probable that the greater portions of the scripts antedated Alijah Billington.

I selected one of these manuscript volumes, not a thick or heavy book, by any means, and sat back to examine it carefully. It bore no title on its cover, which was of a peculiarly smooth leather, and of a texture which suggested human skin; but on one of the inner sheets, preceeding some script which began immediately thereafter, without preamble, appeared the legend: *Al Azif—Ye Booke of Ye Arab.* I leafed rapidly through it, and decided that it was composed of fragmentary translations from some other text or texts, at least one of which was in Latin, and one in Greek. Moreover, there were plainly seen creases in many of the sheets, and annotations in themselves cryptic—'Br. Museum,' 'Bib. Nationale,' 'Widener,' 'Univ. Buenos Aires,' 'San Marcos,'—though a little study convinced me that these notes indicated origin, and referred to various famed museums, libraries, and universities in London, Paris, Cambridge, Buenos Aires, and Lima; there occurred also significant dissimilarities in the script, which gave ample evidence that a number of hands had assisted in the compilation. All this plainly suggested that someone—possibly Alijah himself—had been desperately anxious to obtain the essential parts of this book, and had evidently paid various persons to visit the repositories which contained copies of it, for it must have been exceedingly rare, to transcribe pages which he might assimilate and bind for his own shelves. It was manifest, however, that the book was far from complete, and there was little attempt at order, though the annotations indicated that whoever had prepared it for binding had struggled desperately at first to find some coherence in the pages which must have been sent to him from all over the world.

As I was going through its pages for the second time, somewhat more slowly, I caught sight for the first time of one of those names associated with the trouble in the Wood, and held the page, which was in a very thin, spidery script, not easily legible, but scholarly. I turned it closer to the light, and read.

'Never is it to be thought that man is either oldest or last of the Masters of Earth; nay, nor that the great'r part of life and substance walks alone. The Old Ones were, the Old Ones are, and the Old Ones shall be. Not in the spaces known to us, but *between them,* They walk calm and primal, of no dimensions, and to us unseen. Yog-Sothoth knows the gate, for Yog-Sothoth is the gate. Yog-Sothoth is the key and the guardian of the gate. Past, present, future—what has been, what is, what will be, all are one in Yog-Sothoth. He knows where the Old Ones broke through of old, and where They shall break through in time to come until the Cycle is complete. He knows why no one can behold Them as They walk. Sometimes men can know Them near by Their smell, which is strange to the nostrils, and like unto a creature of great age; but of Their semblance no man can know, save seldom in features of those They have begotten on mankind, which are awful to behold, and thrice awful are Those who sired them; yet of those Offspring there are divers kinds, in likeness greatly differing from man's truest image and fairest eidolon to that shape without sight or substance which is Them. They walk unseen, They walk foul in lonely places where the Words have been spoken and the Rites howled through at Their Seasons, which are in the blood and differ from the seasons of man. The winds gibber with Their voices; the Earth mutters with Their consciousness. They bend the forest. They raise up the waves. They crush the city—yet not forest or ocean or city beholds the hand that smites. Kadath in the cold waste knows them, and what man knows Kadath? The ice desert of the South and the sunken isles of Ocean hold stones whereon Their seal is engraven, but who has seen the deep frozen city of the sealed tower long garlanded with seaweed and barnacles? Great Cthulhu is Their cousin, yet can he spy Them only dimly. As a foulness shall They be known to the race of man. Their hands are at the throats of men forever, from beginning of known time to end of time known, yet none sees Them; and Their habitation is even one with your guarded threshold. Yog-Sothoth is the key to the gate whereby the spheres meet. Man rules now where once They ruled; soon They shall rule again where man rules now. After summer is winter, and after winter summer. They wait patient and potent, for here shall They reign again, and at Their coming again none shall dispute Them and all shall be subject to Them. Those who know of the gates shall be impelled to open the way for Them and shall serve Them as They desire, but those who open the way unwitting shall know but a brief while thereafter.'

There followed an hiatus, and soon another page began. But this was in another hand, from another source; it appeared to be of much older origin than the page I had just read, for not only was the paper itself yellower, but the script was almost archaic.

' 'Twas done then as it had been promis'd aforetime, that He was tak'n by Those Whom He Defy'd, and thrust into ye Neth'rmost Deeps und'r ye Sea, and placed within ye barnacl'd Tower that is said to rise amidst ye great ruin that is ye Sunken City (R'lyeh), and seal'd within by ye Elder Sign, and, rag'g at Those who had imprison'd Him, He furth'r incurr'd Their anger, and They, descend'g upon him for ye second time, did impose upon Him yᵉ semblance of Death, but left Him dream'g in that place under yᵉ great waters, and return'd to that place from whence they had come, Namely, Glyu-Vho, which is among yᵉ stars, and looketh upon Earth from yᵉ time when yᵉ leaves fall to that time when yᵉ ploughman becomes habit'd once again to his fields. And there shall He lie dream'g forever, in His House at R'lyeh, toward which at once all His minions swam and strove against all manner of obstacles, and arrang'd themselves to wait for His awaken'g powerless to touch yᵉ Elder Sign and fearful of its great pow'r know'g that yᵉ Cycle returneth, and He shall be freed to embrace yᵉ Earth again and make of it His Kingdom and defy yᵉ Elder Gods anew. And to His brothers it happen'd likewise, that They were tak'n by Those Whom They Defy'd and hurl'd into banishment, Him Who Is Not to Be Nam'd be'g sent into Outermost space, beyond yᵉ Stars and with yᵉ others likewise, until yᵉ Earth was free of Them, and Those Who Came in yᵉ shape of Towers of Fire, return'd whence They had come, and were seen no more, and on all Earth then peace came was unbrok'n while Their minions gather'd and sought means and ways with which to free yᵉ Old Ones, and waited while man came to pry into secret, forbidd'n places and open yᵉ gate.'

I turned resolutely to the next sheet, which was somewhat smaller in size, and on an onion-skin paper, and bore every sign of having been written surreptitiously, perhaps under the eye of some watcher, for the writer had made all manner of abbreviation, so that it was necessary to pause from time to time, what with the added difficulty of his script, to figure out what it was that he wrote. This third entry appeared to follow the second more closely than the second half had followed the initial sheet I had read.

'Concern'g yᵉ Old Ones, 'tis writ, they wait ev'r at yᵉ Gate, & yᵉ Gate is all places at all times, for They know noth'g of time or place but are in all time & in all place togeth'r without appear'g to be, & there are those amongst Them which can assume divers Shapes & Featurs & any Giv'n Shape & any giv'n Face & yᵉ Gates are for Them ev'rywhere, but yᵉ 1st. was that which I caus'd to be op'd, Namely, in Irem, yᵉ City of Pillars, yᵉ city under yᵉ desert, but wher'r men sett up yᵉ Stones and sayeth thrice yᵉ forbidd'n Words, they shall cause there a Gate to be establish'd & shall wait upon Them Who Come through yᵉ gate, ev'n as Dhols, & yᵉ Abomin. Mi-Go, & yᵉ Tcho-Tcho peop., & yᵉ Deep Ones, & yᵉ Gugs, & yᵉ Gaunts of yᵉ Night & yᵉ Shog-goths, & yᵉ Voormis, & yᵉ Shantaks which guard Kadath in yᵉ Colde Waste & yᵉ Plateau Leng. All are alike yᵉ Children of yᵉ Elder Gods, but yᵉ Great Race of Yith & yᵉ Gt. Old Ones fail'g to agree, one with another, & boath with yᵉ Elder Gods, separat'd, leav'g yᵉ Gr. Old Ones in possession of yᵉ Earth, while yᵉ Great Race, return'g from Yith took up Their Adobe forward in Time in Earth-Land not yet known to those who walk yᵉ Earth today, & there wait till there shall come again yᵉ winds & yᵉ Voices which drove Them forth before & That which Walketh on yᵉ Winds over yᵉ Earth & in yᵉ spaces that are among yᵉ Stars for'r.'

Here there occurred a break of some proportions, as if what had been written there had been carefully ex-punged, though how, I could not see, for the paper revealed nothing. A short paragraph concluded the excerpt.

'Then shal They return & on this great Return'g shal yᵉ Great Cthulhu be fre'd from R'lyeh beneath yᵉ Sea & Him Who Is Not To Be Nam'd shal come from His City which is Carcosa near yᵉ Lake of Hali, & Shub-Niggurath shal come forth & multiply in his Hideous-ness, & Nyarlathotep shal carry yᵉ word to all the Gr. Old Ones & their Minions, & Cthugha shal lay His Hand upon all that oppose Him & Destroy, & yᵉ blind idiot, yᵉ noxious Azathoth shal arise from yᵉ middle of yᵉ World where all is Chaos & Destruction where He hath bubbl'd & blasphem'd at Yᵉ centre which is of All Things, which is to say Infinity, & Yog-Sothoth, who is y⁰ All-in-One & One-in-All, shal bring his globes, & Ithaqua shal walk again, & from y⁰ black-litt'n caverns within y⁰ Earth shal come Tsathoggua, & togeth'r shal take possession of Earth and all things that live upon it, & shal prepare to do battle with y⁰ Elder Gods when y⁰ Lord of y⁰ Great Abyss is apprised of their return'g & shal come with His Brothers to disperse y⁰ Evill.'

The afternoon was now coming to an end, and, though filled with a strange conviction that within these ancient pages lay the key to the mystery, even though it was not given to me to understand it correctly, the waning light and my cousin's activity in the kitchen forced me to abandon the reading for the time being. I put the book aside, my perplexity very great in the face of these sinister and terrible allusions to something apparently primordial and completely beyond my ken; I was convinced that this compilation of fragments had been begun at the instigation of that Richard Billington who had been 'destroy'd by the Thing he call'd out of the Sky,' and continued at the direction of Alijah, but to what end was not apparent, unless it was to add to their store of a knowledge which must certainly have been forbidden to mankind. The implications of the Billingtons having known how properly to interpret what they read and how to use that knowledge were terrible, especially so in the light of the events which had been contemporaneous with their existence.

At I turned away and rose to make my way to the kitchen my eyes involuntarily sought the leaded window, and I received a profound and frightening shock, for the last red sunlight lay upon the stained glass in such a way as to outline in that place an unutterably hideous caricature of an inhuman face of some great, grotesque being whose features were horribly distorted, eyes—if such there were—sunken into pits, without anything resembling a nose, though there seemed to be nostrils; a bald and gleaming head, the entire lower half of which terminated in a mass of writhing tentacles; and at the same time that I gazed in horror at this apparition, I was conscious once again of an overpowering malignance, and once more that terrible awareness of evil smote me from all sides, pressing down upon me like something sentient flowing from walls and windows, as if eager to destroy all life within its range—and briefly, too, it seemed, my nostrils were assailed by a noxious stench, a charnel odour which was the epitome of all that was nauseating and frightful.

Shaken though I was, I resisted the impulse to close my eyes and turn away, but continued to gaze at the window, certain that I was the victim of an hallucination, doubtless given substance by what I had been reading; whereupon the hideous image diminished and faded, the window resumed its normal appearance, and the horrible smell in my nostrils impinged no more. But what next took place was in a way even more terrifying, and I invited its occurrence.

Not content with having proved to myself that I had been made the victim of an optical illusion which had previously frightened my cousin Ambrose, I climbed once more to the top of the case below the window, and looked through the central pane, the uncoloured pane, in the direction of the stone tower, which I confidently expected to see, as before, outlined among the trees in the pale light of the setting sun. But, to my unutterable horror, I looked instead upon a landscape completely alien to me, completely foreign to anything within my experience. I almost fell from the case where I knelt, but I held myself with my face turned outward, for the landscape before my eyes was pitted and torn, and was assuredly non-terrestrial, and the sky overhead was filled with strange, baffling constellations, of which I knew none save one, very close, which bore a resemblance to the Hyades, as if that group had come closer to earth by thousands upon thousands of light years. And there was movement in what I saw—movement in those alien heavens, movement on that blasted landscape, as of great, amorphous beings which came rapidly towards me with manifestly evil intent, grotesque octopoid representations, and awful things that flew on great black rubbery wings and dragged repellent claw-like feet.

My head reeling, I turned away and climbed back down; but at once, surrounded again by the prosaic setting of the study, the reaction came; I climbed back up, nerving myself all the way, and once more applied my eyes to that circle of plain window—and saw what I had expected in the beginning to see—the tower and the trees and the setting sun. But it was a considerably subdued man who made his way back to the study floor. I might be able to write off my impression of the hideous face in the leaded window as an hallucination; but what was there left to say of what I had seen through that glass? I realized instantly that I could not tell Ambrose of what I had seen; he might readily believe me, and thus aggravate his own condition. If indeed I had seen what I felt certain I had, upon what landscape had I looked, what place, what corner of the universe that it could be so frightfully alien and terrible?

I stood for a few moments beneath the window, gazing up at it from time to time, half-expecting to see again that horrible metamorphosis, but nothing happened. I was aroused at last from my contemplation by the sound of my cousin's voice calling me to the evening meal, and, shouting an answer, I left the study —not without a last fearful glance over my shoulder for the now darkening pane—and made my way to the kitchen where Ambrose waited before the repast he had prepared.

'Did you find anything in his books?' asked Ambrose.

Something in the tone of his voice gave me pause. I glanced at him, and saw that his expression was, while not hostile, certainly not friendly, and I divined that his question was in the nature of one seeking information it would not be wise to give. Yet I answered him truthfully enough, that I had read here and there, and could understand nothing whatsoever of what I had read.

This semed to satisfy him, yet there was evident that inner conflict of which he was himself aware, if momentary puzzlement of his features was any indication. I offered nothing more, however, nor did he; so we passed through the meal in silence.

Both of us, being tired, sought our rooms early that night.

I had resolved to broach the subject of Ambrose's coming to spend the winter with me in Boston, and I saw by the light snow which had begun to fall, that I must do so at the earliest opportunity; yet, that opportunity would not come until I could be assured that my cousin was once more amenable to such suggestion, and that he would not be so long as he appeared in any way hostile to me.

The surroundings were quiet, the only sound being the sifting of the snow-flakes upon the window-panes, and I was soon asleep. Sometime in the night, however, I was awakened by what I took to be the slamming of a door. I sat up to listen, but heard nothing more; and, thinking that my cousin might again have gone out, I got up then, quietly, and crossed the hall to his room. Trying the door, I found it open, and entered silently; but my silence was to no account, since Ambrose had indeed gone out. My first impulse was to follow him, but this I deemed unwise, after due thought, for in the snow it was possible for him to see my footprints; by the same token, it would be quite possible for me to follow his tracks in the morning, since the snow had ceased to fall. I lit a match and consulted my watch; it was two o'clock in the morning.

I was about to return to my own room when I was conscious of an alien sound—of music! I listened and heard a strange flute-like playing, for the most part in minor key, which was accompanied by a humming or throbbing or chanting as of a human voice. This rose, as nearly as I could determine, from somewhere west of the house; and I opened the window in my cousin's room a trifle to satisfy myself that this was so, and,

110

having satisfied myself, closed it again. I was more than ever impelled to follow my cousin and ascertain what he did, consciously or in sleep, but caution stayed my footsteps—caution, and a residual memory of what had happened to certain other pryers in time past who had followed someone into the wood.

I returned to my own room and lay awake, waiting for Ambrose to return, fearful that something might have happened to him. But in somewhat less than two hours he was back; I heard the door close, less loudly this time, and I heard my cousin's deliberate footsteps on the stairs. He entered his room and closed the door behind him, after which there was silence once more, save for the distant hooting of an owl; this also was suddenly cut off in the midst of a call, and once again night and silence closed down upon the house.

In the morning I arose before Ambrose. I let myself out by the front door, since I had seen that he had gone by the back, and made a meandering circuit into the woods to meet his tracks, which, as I had suspected, led to the stone tower on the one-time island. I followed his tracks easily enough. The amount of snow that had fallen was approximately an inch, and in this his path lay as clearly marked as I dared to hope it might be. The track, as I had said, led directly to the tower, and into it. Moreover, because of the snow which had entered through the opening Ambrose had made in the roof, it was possible to see that his tracks led not only into the tower, but up the sidewall steps to the platform below the opening. I followed the same path without hesitation, and presently found myself standing where Ambrose had stood and looking out towards the house, which was visible, outlined against the rising sun on its little knoll. Having discovered the house, I lowered my eyes to look for any sign of what my cousin had been doing at the tower, and, in so doing, I saw curiously disturbing marks in the snow beyond the tower. I stared at them for a few moments, unable to determine what they were, and then, dreading what I might find, I descended the stairs, left the tower, and made my way to them.

There were three distinct types of marks, and each was fraught with suggestive horror. There was first a large indentation in the snow, approximately twelve feet in length by some twenty-five feet across, which had the appearance as of some elephantine creature's pausing there; the air being reasonably cold, and no thaw having set in, I examined the outer edges of this depression, and was able to ascertain that whatever it was had sat there had had a smooth skin. The second type of mark was claw-like, of the dimensions of approximately three feet across and the suggestion of being webbed; and the third was a sinister brushed patch on the snow, framing the claw-marks, as if great wings had flapped there—but what manner of wings was not apparent. I stood gazing at these marks in mounting stupefaction, for their portent was almost unmistakable, though against all reason, and, having had my shocked fill of them, I retreated the way I had come, diverging from my cousin's path as soon as possible, and returning to the house in a very round-about way indeed, lest he become suspicious of my absence.

Ambrose was up, as I had thought he would be, and I was relieved to see that he was again himself. He was very weary, and somewhat querulous; he had missed me; he was tired, which he could not understand, for he had certainly slept soundly during the night; he was aware of a feeling of oppression. Moreover, he said, since he had missed me, he had gone around looking for me, and had discovered that we had had a visitor in the night, who had come to the back door and left again, apparently unable to arouse us. I understood instantly that he had seen his own tracks but had not recognized them, and by this knew that he had not been awake during his nocturnal visit to the tower.

I explained that I had gone for a short walk. It was my custom to do so in the city, and I disliked to vary that custom too much.

'I don't know what's the matter with me,' he complained. 'I don't feel at all like getting breakfast.'

'Let me do it,' I suggested, and immediately got to work at it.

He assented readily enough, and sat down, rubbing his forehead with one palm. 'I seem to have forgotten something. Were we planning to do anything today?'

'No. You're just tired, that all.' I thought that now was as good a time as any to propose his winter visit to my Boston home; moreover, I was myself eager to escape this house, being now horribly aware of evil and active danger. 'Hasn't it ever occurred to you, Ambrose, that you need a change of scene?'

'I have hardly settled into this one,' he answered.

'No, I mean a temporary change. Why not spend this winter with me in Boston? Then, if you like, I'll come up with you again in the spring. You can study, if you like, at the Widener; there are lectures and concerts, and what's more, there are people to meet and talk with, which you need. Any man does, I don't care who he is.'

He was dubious, but he was not opposed to the idea, and I knew then that it was but a matter of time before he would consent. I was jubilant, but with caution, for I knew that I must press my advantage before his hostile mood returned and he was aroused against the idea, as he surely would be; so I kept at him relentlessly all morning, not forgetting to suggest that some of the Billington books be taken along with us for winter study, and finally, shortly after lunch, he agreed to spend the winter in Boston; and, having agreed, was so eager to get away—as if motivated by a deep-seated sense of self-preservation—that by nightfall we were actually on the way.

Late in March we returned from Boston, Ambrose with a curious eagerness, myself with apprehension, though it must be admitted, apart from a few uneasy nights at first, during which my cousin walked somnambulistically about as if he were lost, Ambrose had been very much himself throughout the winter months, and had put forward nothing whatever in his conduct or conversation to give me the slightest reason to feel that he had not fully recovered from the oppression which had caused him initially to send for me. As a matter of record, Ambrose was socially very popular, and it was I who, lost in those queer old books from Alijah Billington's library, proved to be somewhat lacking in the social graces. Throughout the winter, I applied myself diligently to these books; there were many more passages similar to those I have set down; there were many references to the key-names which I had come to know; there were some apparently contradictory passages also—but there was nowhere any clear, concise statement of basic credo sufficiently clear to warrant acceptance, nor was there anything like an outline of the pattern to which these monstrous allusions and sinister inferences belonged.

As the spring approached, however, my cousin had become somewhat more restless and more than once expressed a desire to return to the house in Billington's Wood, which, as he pointed out, was after all his 'home,' where he 'belonged'—this was in contrast to his indifference to certain aspects of the manuscript volumes I had sought to discuss from time to time during the winter. Only two things of any moment took place during the winter, concerning the occurrences in the vicinity of Billingtons Wood, and these were duly reported in the Boston newspapers—these were the discovery of the bodies of two victims of uncanny vanishings from the Dunwich country, the discovery being made at different times, one of them between Christmas and New Year's day of that winter, the other shortly after the first of February. As before, both bodies were found to have been dead but a short while, both appeared to have been dropped from a height, varying between them, both were badly mangled and torn, however recognizable, and in each case several months had intervened between the time of disappearance and the time of discovery. The papers made much of the fact that no ransom notes had ever turned up, and stressed the additional fact that the victims had had no reason to leave home, and no trace of them between the time of their vanishing and the finding of their bodies—one on an island in the Miskatonic, the other near the mouth of that river—had been recorded or uncovered, despite the diligence of newspapermen assigned to the case. I saw with some chilling fascination that my cousin seemed to take a *bewildered* interest in these accounts; he read them over and over, but throughout with the air of a man who feels he should know the hidden meaning of what he reads, but had somehow forgotten the proper bridge to remembrance.

I viewed this with an alarm which was, because I was incapable of understanding its meaning, fundamentally not perceptive. I have already set down that my cousin's restlessness, as spring approached, developing into an eager desire to return to the house he had quitted to accompany me to Boston, filled me with misgivings and apprehension, and there is nothing to be gained by delaying the admission that my apprehension was soon justified, for almost at once on our return, my cousin began to act in a manner completely antipodal to his conduct as my winter-guest in the city.

We arrived at the house in Billington's Wood just after sunset of an evening in late March—a mild, mellow evening, the air of which was redolent with the perfumes of flowering sap, leafing trees and flowering plants, and bore upon the light east wind a pleasant pungence of smoke. We had hardly completed our unpacking before my cousin came from his room in high degree of excitement. He would have passed me by, if I had not caught him by the arm.

'What is it, Ambrose?' I asked.

He gave me an immediate, hostile glance, but answered civilly enough. 'The frogs—do you hear them? Listen to them sing!' He pulled his arm away. 'I'm going outside to listen to them. They're welcoming me back.'

I suppose I had been subconsciously aware of the chorus of the frogs ever since our return, but Ambrose's reaction was alarmingly calculated to make me extremely cognizant. Divining that my company would be unwelcome, I did not follow my cousin; instead I went to his room across the hall and sat down at one of his windows, which was open, recalling swiftly that it was at this window that Laban had sat a century ago wondering about his father and the Indian, Quamis. The din of the frogs was really deafening—it rang in my ears, it rang in the room; it pulsed up out of that strange marshy meadow in the midst of the wood between the stone tower and the house. But as I sat listening to that deafening clamour, I was aware of something even more odd than the clamour itself.

In most areas of the temperate zone none but the hylidae—the peepers, the cricket frogs, and the tree frogs chiefly—and an occasional wood frog, calls before April, except in case of unusually mild weather, which the first week of spring had not been. Following the hylidae come the ranae, and, after them, finally, the bull-frogs. Yet, in the melée of sound rising from that marsh I could pick out with ease the voices of peepers, cricket frogs, tree frogs, toads, brown frogs, pond frogs, pickerel and leopard frogs—and even bull-frogs! My initial astonishment was tempered by the instant conviction that the clamour was so great that my auditory sense had been deceived; I had often had the experience of mistaking the shrill, piping notes of spring peepers in late April for the calling of a distant whippoorwill, and I thought this an auditory illusion of like nature; but I soon found that it was not, for I was easily able to isolate the various voices and typical notes and songs!

There was no possibility of an error, and this was most curiously disturbing. It was disturbing not alone because it was something contrary to the pattern of nature as I had become familiar with it, but because of certain abstruse allusions to the behaviour of amphibian life in the presence or proximity of either the outlandishly named 'Beings' of manuscript books in which I had read, or their followers, which is to say, their servitors or worshippers, which were often synonymous, the behaviour of the amphibia being such as to give evidence of their singular awareness, which was present, hinted that writer described only as the 'mad Arab,' because the amphibia were of the same primal relationship as the sect of followers of the Sea-Being known as the 'Deep Ones.' The writer had intimated, in short, that the terrestrial amphibia were both unusually active and unusually vocal in the presence of their primal relatives, 'be they visible or invisible, to them it maketh no difference, for they feel them, & give voice.'

I listened, therefore, to that appalling choir with feelings which were badly mixed—I had had all winter a certain assurance in my cousin's conduct, which had truly been the height of social normalcy; now it would seem that his reversion had been instant and far more complete than before, being complete in the sense that it had been accomplished without either struggle or manifest distress; indeed, Ambrose had seemed well pleased to hear the frogs, and this in turn reminded me with the clarion alarm of bells of that adjuration in Alijah Billington's curious 'instructions'—*He is not to disturb the forgs, particularly the bull-frogs of the marshland between the tower and the house, nor the fireflies, nor the birds known as whip-poor-wills, lest he abandon his locks and guards.* The suggestion inherent in this adjuration was not pleasant, in any way it might be regarded; if the frogs and the fireflies and the whip-poorwills were 'his'—presumably Ambrose's—'locks and guards,' then what did this clamour signify? Was it meant to warn Ambrose that 'something' invisible stood near, or that some alien intruder stood by?—an alien intruder who could then only be myself!

I drew away from the window and went resolutely out of the room, down the stairs, and out to where my cousin stood with his arms folded across his chest, his head tilted back slightly, so that his chin was outthrust, and a strange light glowing in his eyes. I came up to him resolved to challenge his pleasure, but at sight of him, my determination wavered and faded, and I stood at his side, saying nothing, until his continued silence troubled me and I asked him if he enjoyed the choir of voices in the fragrant evening.

Without turning to me he replied enigmatically, 'Soon the whippoorwills will sing, too, and the fireflies will shine—and that will be the time.'

'For what?'

He did not answer and I moved back. In so doing, I caught sight of movement in the deepening dusk on that side of the house facing the driveway into the place, and, acting on impulse, I ran quickly in that direction— I had been a sprinter in my school days, and had lost only a little of my running ability—with the result that, just as I rounded the house, I saw an inconceivably ragged individual vanishing into the scrub growth along the side of the drive on his way out of the wood. I gave chase at once, and soon caught up with him, catching him by one arm as he ran. I found myself holding on to a young man of perhaps twenty or thereabouts, who tried desperately to tear himself loose.

'Leave me go!' he half-sobbed. 'I ain't done nothin'.'

'What were you doing?' I asked sternly.

'Jist wanted to see if He was back, an' I seed 'im. They said he was back.'

'Who said?'

'Can't ye hear? The frogs—that's who!'

I was shaken, and in my involuntary reaction, I held him tighter than I meant to do, so that he cried out in pain. Relaxing my grip a little, I demanded his name under promise of freeing him.

'Don't ye tell 'im,' he begged.

'I won't.'

'I'm Lem Whately, that's who.'

I released him, and he darted away at once, clearly not believing that I did not mean to pursue him again. But, seeing that I had indeed meant what I had said, he hesitated some twenty yards away, turned, and came hurriedly back, making no sound. He caught hold of my coat-sleeve urgently, and in a low voice commanded my attention.

'Ye doan't ack like one of *them,* ye doan't. Better git aout a here afore anythin' happens.'

Then he darted away once more, but this time he was really gone, vanishing with consummate ease into the growing darkness now shrouding the woods. Behind me the clamour of the frogs still rose to maddening proportions, and I was grateful that my room opened on to the east side of the house, away from the marsh; even so, the choir would be audible enough. But, fully as loudly ringing in my ears, were Lem Whately's words, which had aroused a feeling of unreasonable terror within me, terror which lies always in wait in any man faced with the unknown, and is inextricably bound up with the urgency towards flight in the face of the inexplicable. I managed, after a few moments, to quell this terror and also the impulse to heed Lem Whately's adjuration, and turned back towards the house, turning over and over in mind the problem of the Dunwich people—for this new occurrence added on to everything else served to convince me that some further key to the things which were taking place here might be found among those people, and, if I could manage to obtain my cousin's car, it might be worth while to pursue inquiries of my own in that region beyond Dean's Corners.

Ambrose still stood where I had left him; he did not seem to have noticed my absence at all, and, so concluding, I refrained from rejoining him, but repaired to the house, where he presently joined me.

'Surely it is unusual for so many frogs to call so early in the year?' I asked.

'Not here,' he said again, curtly, as if to say that this would put an end to the matter.

I had no wish to continue, for I felt as if my cousin were growing visibly stranger before my eyes, and his hostility was far too easily aroused; by pressing the issue, I might well have aroused more than hostility, and he might summarily show me the door, at the thought of which I realized quite clearly that in large part I would be quite willing to take my leave of him, but duty compelled me to stand by as long as it was possible to do so.

That evening was passed in a strained silence, and I took the first opportunity to retire to my room. Instinct warned me that I had better not turn at this time to those old books in the library; so I took yesterday's paper, picked up in Arkham, instead, and settled down in my room to read it. As it happened, that was not a wise choice, for the paper contained an anonymous account on the editorial page, in a space devoted to letters from readers, to the effect that there was an old woman in Dunwich who had several times been awakened in the night by the voice of Jason Osborn. Now, Osborn was one of the disappearance victims whose bodies had been found during the winter; he had vanished just prior to my coming to visit Ambrose in the first place; and an autopsy performed on the body had indicated that Osborne had been subjected to severe temperature changes, wherever he had been, but that otherwise nothing but the curious mangling and tearing of the flesh had been discovered as an indication of the cause of death. The anonymous lettter-writer was not particularly literate, and charged that the old lady's story had been 'suppres'd' because it 'seeme'd beyond belief' and went on at some length to describe how the old lady had got up and answered and looked in vain for the source of the voice which she heard clearly, and decided finally that it came from somewhere 'beside her, or out of the space or the sky overhead.'

This account fascinated me, for several reasons. In

the first place, it was curiously parallel to the oft-repeated conclusion that not only the body of Osborn, but of others preceding him, appeared to 'have been dropped from a height'; in the second, it brought Dunwich into the problem again; and finally, it added an oblique kind of corroboration to the entire structure of the puzzle—from the adjurations of Alijah Billington and the sinister reference to calling something 'out of the Sky' to the actual happenings of recent date. But at the same time that it impressed me as something of value in the maze where I walked, I was aware, too, of an increasing sense of malignance, as if the very walls watched me, and the house waited for any overt move as an excuse to pounce. Moreover, I found that the account troubled my consciousness; I could not readily get to sleep, and I lay for many hours listening to the clamour of the frogs, listening to the restless tossing of my cousin in the room across the hall, listening for something more and hearing—was it dream or waking? —sounds as of great footsteps walking under the earth and in the heavens.

The frogs cried and sang all night long; there was no surcease until the dawn, and even then a few batrachian voices still rose in croaking calls. When at last I rose and dressed, I was still tired, but I had not retreated an inch from my determination of the previous night—to visit Dunwich if I could.

So immediately after breakfast I pressed my cousin to permit my use of his car, pleading a necessity to go into Arkham. He assented readily and, I thought, with a sense of relief, so that he became almost genial, with a geniality which seemed even more marked when I said somewhat hesitantly that I might find it expedient to be gone for the entire day. He himself conducted me to the car and saw me off, urging me to stay in Arkham as long as I liked, and use the car as much as I needed it.

Despite the impulsiveness of my decision, I had my initial objective well in mind. It was that same old

Mrs. Bishop whose curiously oblique conversation my cousin had roughly summarized for me in one of our first conversations, and who, in her mutterings, had spoken of Nyarlathotep and Yog-Sothoth. From what Ambrose had set down on the back of an envelope among the papers he had permitted me to see, I felt that I could find my way to her abode without difficulty, and without any need to stop and inquire the way. Moreover, since, according to my cousin's account, she was apparently a superstitious, if cunning, old woman I had hit upon what I felt was a bold stroke—I would approach her as obliquely as possible in an effort to draw from her something she might not otherwise say.

I found the place as easily as I had expected. The low house with the faded white siding identified itself from my memory of my cousin's description; and the gate-post scrawled with the name 'Bishop' settled any doubt that might have lingered. I went in along the path and across the porch without hesitation, and knocked.

'Come in,' came a cracked voice from within.

I entered the house, and found myself, as my cousin had done, in a darkened room. I made out the figure of the old woman readily enough, and saw that she held on her lap a black cat of some size.

'Set, Stranger.'

I did as she invited me to do, and, without naming myself, I asked, 'Mrs. Bishop—have you heard the frogs in Billington's Wood?'

Without hesitation she replied. 'Aye. I been a-hearin' 'em a-callin' steady, an' I know they're a-callin' fer Them from Outside.'

'You know what it means, Mrs. Bishop.'

'Aye, an' so dew yew, by the sound of ye. Aye—the Master's back. I knew he was a-comin' when the house got opened agin. The Master was a-waitin', an' he was a-waitin' a long time. Now he's come back, an' Them things hes come back, too, a-rippin' an' a-tearin' an' Lord knows what all. I'm an old woman, Stranger, an' I ain't long tew live, but I ain't hopin' tew die thet way. Who are ye a-comin' an' a-askin' these here questions, Stranger? Are yew one a Them?'

'Do I have the marks?' I countered.

'Thet yew doan't. But they can come in any shape They like, that yew know.' Her voice, which had begun to cackle with laughter, suddenly faded. ' 'Tis the same car the Master come in—yew come from the Master!'

'From but not for,' I replied quickly.

She seemed to hesitate. 'I ain't done no wrong. 'Twasn't me writ thet letter. Thet was Lem Whately, a-listenin' to talk not meant fer him.'

'When did you hear Jason Osborn?'

'Ten nights after he was took, an' then twelve nights more, an' then the last time four nights before they found him—like all them others afore my time—an' like Them that'll come after, too. Heard him jest es plain's if he was a-standin' where you're a-settin', Stranger, an' I ain't lived across the valley from Osborn all my life without a-knowin' his voice when I hear it.'

'What did he say?'

'Singin' the first time—words I ain't never heard afore, strange words. The last time it sounded like prayin'. The middle time it was quick-spoke' words in thet language They use—ain't meant fer mortal man.'

'And where was he?'

'Outside. He was Outside with Them, an' They were a-bidin' Their time afore They got ready to eat him.'

'But he wasn't eaten, Mrs. Bishop. He was found.'

'Aye!' She tittered. ' 'Tain't always the flesh They wants—but it's always the sperit or whatever it is thet makes a man think an' figure things out an' what makes him dew an' say things.'

'The life force.'

'Call it what yew will, Stranger. Thet's what They wants, the devils! Aye, he was found, was Jason Osborn—all torn an' mangled, they said—but he was dead, and They'd had Their fill of him, They thet carried him along where They went.'

'And where is that, Mrs. Bishop?'

'Here an' yender, Stranger. They're here all the time, all 'round us, but yew can't see 'em. They're a-listenin' to us talk, might be, an' They' a-waitin' at the door fer the Master tew call Them es he called Them afore. Aye, he's come back, he's come back o'er two hundred years, the way my grandfather said he would, an' he's let Them loose agin an' They're a-flyin' an' a-crawlin' an' a-swimmin' an' a-bein' right next door to us where we are, a-waitin' tew come out again an' git started all over agin. Thay know where the doors are, an' They know the Master's voice—but even he ain't safe from Them if he doan't knows all the signs an' the charms an' the locks. But he does, Master does. He knew 'em way back, accordin' to the Word come down.'

'Alijah?'

'Alijah?' She tittered her obscene laughter into the room. 'Alijah knew more'n mortal man; he knew suthin' nobody can tell. He could call It an' talk to It an' It never got Alijah. Alijah shut It up an' got away. Alijah shut It up—an' he shut up the Master, too, out there, Outside, when the Master was ready tew come back again after thet long a time. Ain't many as knows it, but Misquamacus fer one. Master walked the earth an' none knew him as saw him fer he was in many faces. Aye! He wore a Whately face an' he wore a Doten face an' he wore a Giles face an' he wore a Corey face, an' he sat among the Whatelys an' the Dotens an' the Gileses an' the Coreys, an' 'twas none who knew him for aught but Whately or Doten or Giles or Corey, an' he ate among 'em an' he bedded among 'em an' he walked an' talked among 'em, but so great he was in his Outsideness thet those he took weakened an' died, not being able to contain him. Only Alijah outsmarted Master—aye, outsmarted him more'n a hundred years after Master was dead.' Her horrible laughter welled forth again, and died away. 'I know, Stranger—I know. I ain't no use to 'em, but I hear 'em talkin' Out There, I hear what They're a-sayin' an' even if I can't understand the words, I know what They're a-sayin', I was born with a caul, an' I can hear Them Out There.'

By this time I was coming quickly around to appreciating my cousin's point-of-view. I was aware of her disturbing sense of secret knowledge, of that feeling of almost contemptuous superiority which Ambrose had noticed; I was convinced that she held a vast store of hidden and forbidden knowledge, even though, as before, I encountered that helpless feeling of being without the essential key to understanding the information which was being offered.

'They're a-waitin' tew come back again over all the earth—it ain't jest here, They're a-waitin' all over—way down inside the earth an' under the water as well as Outside, an' Master's a-helpin'.'

'Have you seen the Master?' I could not help asking.

'Never set eye on him. But I seen the shape he took. They ain't one of us don't know he's back. We knew the signs. They took Jason Osborn, didn't They? They come tew git Lew Waterbury, didn't they? They'll come agin!' she added darkly.

'Mrs. Bishop, who was Jonathan Bishop?'

She cackled again, mirthlessly, with something akin to a bat's sound. 'Yew might well ask. He was my grandfather. He come on tew some uv the secrets an' he thought he knew it all—he took tew it right enough an' he begun tew call It an' he sent It after those who pried an' spied, but he wasn't the Master's equal an' suthin' got him the way others was got. An' Master, they say, n'er lifted a finger tew help him, sayin' he was weak an' had no right tew entreat uv the stones or call out tew the hills an' bring them hellish Things down on us an' make hate tew grow in Dunwich, whereby it happened thet not a Corey an' not a Tyndal but hates the Bishops.'

Everything the old woman said held a horrible significance; the Bishop letters to Alijah Billington faithfully bore out what she now told, and further verification existed, as my cousin had troubled to learn, in the files of the Arkham papers. Whatever the motivation, the manifest facts of the matter were beyond dispute; the papers recorded the disappearance and later finding of Wilbur Corey and Jedediah Tyndal, but made no suggestion of a connection to Jonathan Bishop. But the Bishop letters, presumably never seen by anyone but old Alijah in his time, had made the connection even before Corey had vanished; and now here was the old lady calmly admitting that the Coreys and the Tyndals hated the Bishops—and this surely was for no other reason but that they had rightly guessed Jonathan Bishop's connection to those two unsolved disappearances! I was by this time considerably upset because of the conviction that, had I the proper knowledge at my disposal, I would be obtaining far more information from the old woman than I was actually aware of. Moreover, I was conscious of something infinitely terrible lying beneath her words, something that rang in her tittering laughter, something that seemed actually to have a tangible existence in the room—a vast wealth of secret, primal knowledge that seemed to extend for ages into the past, and threatened to impend for ages in the future, and ugly, evil sentience that dwelt forever in the shadows biding its time to come forth and overwhelm all life.

'You never knew your grandfather?'

'No, never. But I knew all my life what they say abaout him. He was smart, all right, but not smart enough, provin' thet, es they say, a little knowledge is dangerous. He set up a circle uv stones an' he called It an' It come an' Suthin' more come, too, an' took him, an' after thet, Master sent It back an' all the Others, too—back Outside through the circle.' She tittered again. 'Doan't yew knew what runs up thar beyond the hill, Stranger?'

I opened my mouth to venture one of the key-names which had appeared in the old books so frequently, but she hushed me in manifest alarm, which though it was not visible on her features, sounded in her voice.

'Doan't yew speak their names, Stranger. If They're a-listenin', might be They'll come nearer, an' foller yew—unless yew got the Sign.'

'Which Sign?'

'The Sign uv perteckshun.'

I recalled my cousin's account of the two loafers who had accosted him on his exploration of Dunwich, inquiring, whether he had the 'Sign.' Presumably this was the same 'Sign,' though there was apparently some discrepancy. I asked about them.

'It was the other Sign they meant. They're fools; they doan't know what it means; they doan't keer what happens; they think they'll get rich an' powerful—but the Sign ain't what they think it is. Them Outside doan't keer abaout makin' folks rich; all They Keers abaout is comin' back—comin' back an' slavin' us an' mixin' with us an' a-killin' us when They're ready, an' then they wunt hev any use fer them what carries Their Sign 'ceptin' may be if you're powerful as Master is. An' then you belong tew them. I know. 'Tain't court knowin', but I know. I heard Jason Osborn a-screamin' the night it got him, an' Sally Sawyer, who tends house fer her cousin Seth, she heard a rippin' an' a tearin' uv boards when thet Thing busted doawn the shed where Osborn was when It come, an' it was the same with Lew Waterbury. Mis' Frye, she seen tracks, she said, prints bigger'n a elephant 'd make, an' all kinds such prints—like es if they was made by suthin' twicet an' three times as big es a elephant an' with more'n four legs, tew; an' she seen wing marks, tew, in different places, but they jest laughed at her an' said she been dreamin' an' when she tuk 'em thar, tew show 'em first off, wasn't nary a track left—only hyar an' thar suthin' *queer,* like as if the prints 'd been marked aout, so none could see.'

I confess to an almost overpowering clamminess of the skin and prickling of my scalp. The woman spoke so intensely that she seemed little aware of me; evidently everything she had heard, coupled with what she had learned of her own forebear, caused her to brood endlessly about the mysterious and horrible events of the countryside.

'An' the wust uv it is, yew doan't see Them a-tall—but yew can tell when They're near by the smell, the wust smell ever—like suthin' straight aout uv Hell!'

Though I heard and understood her words, I was no longer actively listening. Some of the things she had said were beginning to fit into a pattern, a pattern so suggestive that I sat cold with horror at the thought of even so much as contemplating it seriously. She appeared to reverence the 'Master' and had referred to him as over two hundred years old; now, Alijah Billington could not conceivably have been the object of her reference. Was it, then, Richard Billington—or rather, that elusive person written of by the Rev. Ward Phillips as 'one Richard Bellingham or Bollinhan'?

'By what other name do you know the Master?' I asked.

She grew instantly canny, and her suspicion of me was immediately evident. 'Ain't none knows His name, Stranger. Yew can call him Alijah if ye've a mind tew, or yew can call him Richard, or yew can call him suthin' older'n thet. Master lived here a little while an' then he wen away to live Out There! Then he come back agin, an' then he went Out There agin. An' now he's back. I'm an old woman, Stranger, an' all my life I heard tell uv Master, an' I lived all my years a-waitin' fer him, an' expectin' him back, as 'twas foretold he would come. He's got no name, he's got no place, he comes an' he goes in time an' aout uv time.'

'He must be very old.'

'Old?' She tittered, and her claw-like hand made a scraping sound along the arms of her rocker. 'He's older'n me, he's older'n this house, he's older'n yew—an' all three uv us put together. A year ain't nothin' but a breath tew him, and ten year hardly a clock's tickin'.'

She spoke in riddles I could not penetrate. Yet one thing seemed clear—the trail to Alijah Billington and his activities led farther back into time, perhaps even beyond Richard Billington. Just what, then, was Alijah up to? And why had he suddenly taken leave of his native shores and returned to England, from which land his ancestors had come many decades before? The primary assumption which had seemed to me so self-evident that I had immediately accepted it without cavil—that Alijah had taken himself off, after dismissing the Indian, Quamis, to avoid any further implication in the weird and terrible things that went on in his vicinity—seemed no longer so obvious. But if this were not so, then what indeed was Alijah's motivation for his flight? There was nothing to show that the authorities were even within throwing distance of Alijah as the party responsible for the untoward events of that neighbourhood—specifically, the disappearances and even stranger reappearances.

The old woman was silent now. Somewhere in the house I heard a clock ticking. The cat on her lap stood up, arched its black back, and padded to the floor.

'Who sent yew here, Stranger?' she asked suddenly.

'No one sent me. I came.'

'Came with a reason, yew did. Dew yew belong to the Sheriff's men?'

I assured her that I did not.

'An' yew doan't carry the Elder Sign?'

Again I replied in the negative.

'Take keer whar yew walk, take keer what yew talk, or Them Outside will see yew an' hear yew. Or Master will, an' Master doan't like people tew ask questions or pry raound too much, an' when Master doan't like suthin' Master calls It from the Sky or the hills whare'er It lies.'

I could not help reflecting that, throughout the old

woman's part in our dialogue, I had never once entertained any doubt of her sincerity. She believed quite simply in what she said; she might not herself fully understand all the implications of her words, but she did believe in some alien force which manifested itself in different ways and was malignant in so far as mankind was concerned. Of so much I had not the slightest doubt whatever. She spoke almost religiously at times, and I was somewhat surprised to learn through further questioning, that she was a Congregationalist, even if she did not often get to church, and that she had a staunch belief in God—a belief which was evidently not at all incompatible with her fear of the extra terrestrial beings which had such a vivid and colourful existence in her thoughts.

When at last I took my leave of her, I was convinced that the dark waters in which both my cousin and I were swimming were too shoreless for either of us, or for both of us together. The mild schizophrenia which affected my cousin in his house and wood further complicated the matter, and it was evident that I must turn elsewhere for further assistance, or fail miserably in my quest, and bring to being God knows what forces —for I was now in such a state of mind that, even without understanding them, I was willing to concede the existence of malign forces which lay in wait somewhere in the hills—what manner of creature I knew not—to decimate the ranks of mankind.

My drive home was a very thoughtful one, and I was lost in a maze of many openings but no egresses, presenting a complex of passages, each one of which led to a dead end. It was therefore in a sombre mood that I arrived finally at the house, where I found my cousin busy in the study. He had evidently not thought I would be home so early, for at my entrance he hastily put away the papers on which he had been working, but not before I had glimpsed curious diagrams and charts in his hand. His perplexing secrecy invited my own; I did not offer any explanation of where I had been, and I managed to evade his questions, which was manifestly to his annoyance, though he betrayed this by no word. He seemed, in fact, uncomfortable at my continued presence, and I have no doubt I must have seemed so also to him. Fortunately, the day was well gone and soon came to an end. I took the first opportunity after the evening meal to retire to my room, pleading a headache—which was not far from the truth, if one can concede that the confusion of my thoughts was indeed a psychic turmoil equivalent to a physical headache.

In view of what took place that night, I want to make every effort to show that I was not actually ill or under any abnormal influence. My thoughts were chaotic, yes, but I was not in such a state of mind as to make possible easily accepted delusions. As a matter of fact, I was particularly alert, very possibly because of some instinctive expectation that something untoward might take place at any time.

The evening began, as had the previous one, with the demoniac piping of the frogs, rising to deafening heights in the marsh in the midst of the Wood between the tower and the house; the sun had scarcely gone down, I had not yet gone to my room, when their piping began—not, as the naturalist has come to expect, with a first few tentative calls from here and there, and then a gradually swelling chorus—but rather with a full-bodied choir at once, as if by some prearranged signal, within a few minutes of the sun's disappearance down the western heaven. My cousin affected not to hear their hellish piping, and I made no mention of it; not knowing what he might think if I were to pursue the subject we had undertaken on the previous evening. But in the sanctuary of my room, I was increasingly aware of their piping choir, even though it was less raucous there.

Nevertheless, I was determined to permit my imagination no freedom to roam. I turned with premeditated deliberation to a book I have always carried with me

131

—Kenneth Grahame's *The Wind in the Willows*—and began to read over again the adventures of those lovable characters, Mole, Toad, and Rat, prepared to enjoy them, as always; and in a comparatively short time, considering the demands of the setting and the incidents which had taken place since first I had come in response to my cousin's frantic request, I was lost in the pleasant English countryside along that eternal River which flows through the home country of Grahame's unforgettable characters. Moreover, I read a considerable time, and, though I was never once fully unconscious of that batrachian piping, I was comparatively lost in my book. When finally I put it down, the hour was approaching midnight, and a gibbous moon had swung into the western sky from its earlier position east of the zenith. I put out the light in my room, since my eyes were somewhat tired. Yet I myself was not tired; I was relaxed, a little troubled still in the remote recesses of my mind, from which the events of the story so familiar to me had not yet receded, and in that condition I sat for some time, while the various parts of the Billington puzzle arranged themselves once more before my mind's eye.

While I was striving to find some rationale in the problem, I became aware of the opening of my cousin's door, and of his emergence into the hall. I believe I knew instantly that he was on his way to the stone tower; I remember having the impulse to stop him, but I did not yield to it. I heard him go down the stairs, and then for a while no further sound; and then the closing of an outer door. I crossed the hall into his room, from which I could look down to that expanse of lawn over which Ambrose would have to pass in order to reach the fringe of wooded land between the house and the marsh and tower. I saw him walking there, and again experienced an impulse to set out after him. But I was deterred by more than reason; I was aware of something akin to fear—I had no assurance that my cousin walked in his sleep tonight, as he had done other nights; it was quite possible that he was awake, and, awake, he might certainly have resented actively my dogging his footsteps.

I stood for some time undecided, and then determined that it might be possible to ascertain whether or not Ambrose went to the tower by the comparatively simple expedient of descending to the study and mounting to the leaded window, to look from the plain glass in its centre, which was so focused on the top of the tower that it should be possible to see, in this moonlight, whether or not any figure appeared in the opening Ambrose had effected in the roof. By the time I had come to this conclusion, Ambrose had had ample time in which to reach his objective, if indeed it were the tower; so without hesitation I made my way downstairs in the darkness, having become reasonably familiar with the house during my visit, and directly into the study; so that, coming into view of the leaded window for the first time in darkness, I was amazed and startled anew by the brilliant effect of moonlight on the stained glass, lending to the window a most remarkable and vivid effect as of movement, with a vividness which disseminated something of its reflected glow throughout the study.

I mounted the bookcase, as I had done before, though requiring somewhat more care to do so, and presently stood with my eyes peering through the circle of plain glass in the centre. I have previously set forth the effect of a strange illusion I had experienced when peering through this glass on an earlier occasion. The effect I now achieved was on a similar plane, but at first glance, it had none of the appearance of illusion about it, rather only of undue exaggeration, for the scene which met my eye was indeed the landscape I expected to see, but I saw it in a light which seemed to be more brilliant than that of the moon, though of a similar hue —that is, that effect as of white wine overlying everything, subtly altering shapes, colours, shadows into something alien and strange. Out of this landscape rose the tower—only, it appeared now to be very much closer than it had been at any former time; it seemed, indeed, to be no further away than the edge of the wood; and yet the proportions and perspectives were proper and correct, so that I had at one and the same time this impression of viewing the scene through a magnifying glass and the conviction that all was as it should be.

My attention, however, was not directed at the perspectives or even the increased light over that to be expected from the gibbous moon, but rather at the tower itself. Despite the hour, which was now past midnight, I saw quite clearly that my cousin stood on the little platform on top of the stone steps within the tower; indeed, half his body showed quite clearly in the brightness of that illumined landscape, and at the moment of my first sight of him, he stood with both arms extended towards the heavens in the west, where at this hour shone the stars and constellations of the winter nights, very low on the horizon—Aldebaran in the Hyades, part of Orion, and slightly higher, Sirius, Capella, Castor, and Pollux, as well as the planet Saturn—though these were somewhat dimmed by the proximity of the moon. I saw my cousin far more clearly, as I later realized, than I should have seen him by all the laws of perspective and sight applied to the distance, the time, and the setting, but at the moment this did not occur to me as forcefully as it might otherwise have done for a very vivid reason—because I saw far more than these fundamentals of the setting, which seemed, as it were, little more than a frame for the utterly horrible and frightful visions which presented themselves to my view from the study window.

For my cousin Ambrose was not alone.

There extended outward from him an excrescence— no other word seems as apt—which seemed to have neither beginning nor end, but appeared to be in a state of flux, and yet conveyed the unmistakable impression of being alive; an excrescence, I say, that bore at one and the same time vague resemblances to a serpent, a bat, and a vast, amorphous monster in that stage of the world's growth when creatures had not yet wholly emerged from primal slime. Nor was this alone visible to my sight, for all around Ambrose, on the tower's roof, and in the air above it, were others that defy description. On the roof, as it were one on each side of him, were two toad-like creatures which seemed constantly to be changing shape and appearance, and from whom emanated, by some means I could not distinguish, a ghastly ululation, a piping which was matched only by the shrill choir of the frogs, now risen to a truly cacophonous height. And in the air about him were great viperine creatures, which had curiously distorted heads, and grotesquely great clawed appendages, supporting themselves with ease by the aid of black rubbery wings of singularly monstrous dimensions. Indeed, the sight, which in any ordinary circumstance would have sent me reeling back, was so incredible, that my instant reaction was that I had taken leave of my senses, that my concern about the problem of Billington's Wood and the events of the past years in this area had so affected me that such hallucination as this was only to be expected. It is, of course, as I now see, evidence of the plainest sort that, if I could rationalize to such a degree, the things I saw had an existence quite apart from my imagination.

Furthermore, there was out there at the tower a constant flux and flowing; the bat-winged creatures were sometimes to be seen, and sometimes invisible, abruptly vanishing, as if they slipped away into another dimension; the amorphous flute-players on the roof were now great and monstrous, now small and dwarf-like; and the extension in space before my cousin, which I have described as an excrescence, was so hideously in flux that I could not bear to take my eyes from it, convinced as I was that at any moment this illusion and all else would pass, and present once more the calm, moon-lit landscape as I had expected to see it; and by describing it as 'in flux' I know that I fall far short of adequately describing what took place before my horrified and incredible eyes, for the *Thing,* which first appeared before me as an angular extension into space, with its focal point before my cousin Ambrose at the tower, became in succession a great amorphous mass of changing flesh, squamous as certain snakes, and putting forth and drawing back constantly and without cessation innumerable tentacular appendages of all lengths and shapes; a horrible, blackly furred thing with great red eyes that opened from all portions of its body; a hellish monstrosity which was octopoid in seeming to have become a small, shrivelled mass of torso with tentacles hundreds of times its size and weight which whipped backward in a fanning motion into space, and the ends of which were literally sloughed or melted away into distance, while the empurpled body opened a great eye to look upon my cousin, and disclosed beneath it a great pit of mouth from which issued a terrible, if muted, screaming, at the sound of which the flute-players on the tower and the piping singers in the marsh increased their wild music in unbearable volume, and my cousin gave voice to terrible, ululant sounds which drifted unmistakably to my ears as a horrible mockery of something less than human, and filled me with such terror and abysmal fright as I have never known before, for among the sounds he made, he uttered one of the dread names which had occurred so often, always fraught with terror unbelievable, in the history of this accursed region— '*N'gai, n'gha'ghaa, y'hah—Yog-Sothoth!*'—all this making such an eldritch and bestial tumult that I thought surely all the world must bear it, and fell away from the window, once again overcome by that terrible malignance, flowing towards me not so much this time from the walls as from that strange window.

I tumbled, in short, to the floor, falling on one knee, and for a moment remained in that position, while my senses rallied; then I stood up, shakily, and listened—

fearful of what sounds would reach inward; but I heard nothing, and, now, terribly confused and unable to comprehend what had happened, I began to climb back up to the top of the bookcase, despite the strongest inner urgings to take flight. My thoughts were chaotic; it seemed that I had been subjected to an incredibly ghastly hallucination; I felt that I must look once more towards the stone tower in the Wood. Thus, impelled forward and yet torn backward, I once more achieved my former position, and opened my eyes slowly upon the dread scene.

I saw the tower; I saw the Wood with the moonlight on it, and the moon, too, lowering down the west, and from one of the stars what appeared to be a tenuous wavering line of mist that extended briefly outward and vanished, an ectoplasmic extension, as it were—but of that which had impressed itself indelibly upon my consciousness but a few moments before, I saw nothing whatsoever! The tower stood deserted and, though the frog choir still sounded in rhythmic cadence, all other sound had ceased; there was nothing on or about the tower, and of my cousin Ambrose there was no sign. I stood for a moment with my face pressed to the glass, gazing incredulously out; then I realized that my cousin must be on his way back—might even now be approaching the house—for I had lost all sense of time, and I retreated hastily, with only a quick, furtive, apprehension glance out that circular window at the quiet, deserted scene beyond.

I dropped lightly to the floor, retired from the study, and made my way rapidly up the stairs to my room, which I had barely reached before I heard the sound of the door below, and the approaching footsteps of my cousin. But, listening, I started. What footsteps were these? Surely more than of but one man! And how slowly, how draggingly! And what voices rose in whispers from the foot of the stairs!

'A long time!'—guttural, but undoubtedly my cousin Ambrose's voice.

'Aye, Master.'

'Dost find me changed?'

'Nay, save in thy face and garment.'

'Hast gone far?'

'To Mnar, and Carcosa. And thee, Master?'

'In many places, by many faces. Of time past, and time to come. Speak lightly, for there is danger here. There is an outsider of my blood within these walls.'

'Shall I sleep?'

'Hast need of it?'

'None.'

'Rest, then, and wait. By morning it will be as always.'

'Aye, Master. When thou hast need of me, I will be in the cubicle of the kitchen, as before.'

'Stay. Dost know the year as men mark it?'

'Nay, Master. Have I been long gone? Two years? Ten?'

Ambrose's chuckle was audible and terrible to hear. 'But a breath of time! More than twenty times ten. Great changes have come, even as the Old Ones foresaw and we were given to know. You will see them.'

'Good night, Master.'

'Aye, say it well—a long time since last you spoke it here. Rest well, for we have work to do to make ready for Them and open the way.'

Silence, save for the slowly ascending steps of my cousin. I heard him advance with a casual sound all the more terrible because of its commonplaceness coming after what I had seen—if indeed I had seen anything at all—through the study window, after what I had heard rising from the foot of the stairs—if indeed I had heard that oblique, suggestive dialogue, for already I was beginning to doubt the evidence of my senses! My cousin came on down the hall; he entered his room and closed his door. In a little while I heard the creaking of his bed, and then all was still.

My initial impulse then was to immediate flight—but flight would arouse my cousin's suspicion without satisfying his hostility, and I knew that would be impossible. But together with the impulse came a secondary reaction—the feeling that I was deserting Ambrose. Whatever was destined to take place next, however, I assured myself one thing that must be done; I must see Dr. Harper once more. I must lay before him in chronological sequence everything that had taken place, even to reproducing or copying the documents in my cousin's library. At this post-midnight hour, I had little stomach for such a task; yet I knew it must be done. Before leaving the house, I must manage to prepare a statement for the guidance of anyone whose services might be enlisted to solve the riddle of Billington's Wood—and, yes, of the strange and horrible happenings of Dunwich.

I did not sleep that night.

In the morning I waited until my cousin went downstairs before I left my room, and then I did so with trepidation, fearful of what I might see. My fears, however, were ill-founded; I found Ambrose busy making breakfast. He seemed very cheerful, in fact, and his appearance completely lulled my fears, even if it did nothing whatever to disturb the residue of my nocturnal experience. Moreover, he was singularly voluble. He hoped the choir from the marsh had not kept me awake beyond my usual hour.

I assured him that it had not.

The frogs had been unusually loud, he thought, and perhaps some method might possibly be found to diminish their ranks.

For some reason, his suggestion instantly alarmed me. I could not help reminding him of Alijah's adjuration, whereat he smiled, I thought, most sinisterly and somewhat aloofly, as if to suggest that he now knew what Alijah meant and was not disturbed by it. This unusual reaction further upset me, though I felt it necessary to conceal my feelings.

He went on to say that he would be busy outside the

house for the greater part of the day, and hoped I would not mind his absence. He had discovered work that needed to be done in the woods.

I concealed an immediate elation, for his absence would afford me the opportunity for easy access to the papers in the study; yet I felt that I must put a good face on the matter and at least ask whether I might be of assistance to him.

He smiled. 'Now that is generous of you, Stephen. But as a matter of fact—I forgot to tell you—I have help. I hired a fellow during your absence the other day, and I should tell you about him so that you will not be alarmed. He has a quaint mode of speech, and you will find him peculiar in dress. In fact, he is an Indian.'

My astonishment could not be concealed.

'You seem surprised.'

'I am astounded,' I managed to reply. 'Wherever did you find an Indian in these parts?'

'Ah, he came, and I hired him. One might be surprised at what it is possible to discover in these hills.' He got up and prepared to clear away the dishes, since I was manifestly finished eating, and, turning, added one final damning fact. 'It is a curious coincidence you should appreciate—his name is Quamis.'

3

Narrative of Winfield Phillips

Stephen Bates came to Dr. Seneca Lapham's office on the campus of Miskatonic University shortly before noon on the seventh of April, 1924, at the direction of Dr. Armitage Harper, late of the library staff. He was a man of about forty-seven years of age, well-preserved, and beginning to grey a little. Though he manifestly fought to keep himself well under control, he seemed profoundly disturbed and agitated, and I put him down for a neurotic, a potential hysteric. He carried a bulky manuscript, which was composed of an account in his own hand of certain experiences which had befallen him, and a group of related documents and letters copied by him. Because Dr. Harper had telephoned to announce his coming, he was taken directly in to see Dr. Lapham, who appeared most interested in him, which caused me to assume that his manuscript must concern certain aspects of anthropological research so dear to my employer.

He introduced himself, and was encouraged to tell his story immediately, without preamble. This he proceeded to do without further urging. His story was a somewhat intense and incoherent narrative which, as nearly as I could follow his turgid manner of telling, had to do with cult-survival. It was very soon apparent to me, however, that my own reaction to Bates' story counted for nothing; for the expression on the grave face of my employer—his pursed, grim lips, his narrowed, thoughtful eyes, his wrinkled brow, and, above all, the deep absorption with which he listened, completely unaware of the passing of the lunch hour—gave evidence that he, at least, attached some marked significance to Bates' story, which, now he had begun, poured from him in a flood, and was not halted until he bethought himself of his manuscript, whereupon he stopped short, extended the manuscript, and urged Dr. Lapham to read it at once.

To my further surprise, my employer complied. He opened the parcel almost eagerly, and passed me each sheet as he finished with it. No comment from me was asked, and none given. I read his extraordinary record with growing amazement, made all the keener by the the sight of the occasional trembling of Dr. Lapham's hands. Finishing before I did, something over an hour after he had begun reading the easy, flowing script, my employer gazed intently at our visitor and urged him to complete the tale.

But there was no more, replied Bates. He had told all. It was plain, by their presence, that he had managed to copy the documents relating to the matter—or at least those which he thought pertained to it.

'You were not disturbed?'

'Not once. Only after I was through, my cousin returned. I saw the Indian. He was attired pretty much as I had always been taught to believe the Narragansetts would be attired. My cousin now needed my help.'

'Ah, indeed? What was it he required of you?'

'Why, it seemed that neither he nor the Indian nor the two of them together could manage that marked stone which my cousin had dislodged from the roof of the tower. I had not myself thought it beyond the strength of one man, and said so. My cousin thereupon dared me to lift it. He explained that he wished it transported elsewhere, and buried away from the immediate vicinity of the tower. I had no difficulty in doing as he asked, without any help from him.'

'Your cousin did not lend a hand?'

'No. Nor the Indian.'

My employer handed our visitor pencil and paper. 'Will you make a diagram of the tower's environs and indicate the approximate spot where you buried the stone?'

Somewhat perplexed, Bates did so. Dr. Lapham took it gravely and put it carefully away with the last sheets of the manuscript, which I handed to him. He leaned back, his hands crossed over his waist, his fingertips touching.

'It did not seem queer to you that your cousin did not offer to help?'

'Not at all. We had made a wager. I won it. I would naturally not expect him to help me win it when he had to gain by my losing it.'

'That was all he wanted?'

'Yes.'

'Did you see any evidence of what your cousin had been doing?'

'Oh, yes. He and the Indian seemed to have been cleaning up around the tower. I saw that the claw- and wing-prints I had seen on that previous occasion, had been smoothed out and destroyed. I asked about them, but my cousin said only in an offhand way that I must have fancied I saw them there.'

'Your cousin has a continuing awareness of your interest in the mystery of Billington's Wood, then?'

'Yes, of course.'

'Will you leave this manuscript in my possession for the time being, Mr. Bates?'

He hesitated, but finally assented, if it would in any way serve my employer, who assured him that it would. Still, he seemed reluctant to part with it, and was particularly anxious that it be not shown. All this Dr. Lapham promised him.

'Is there anything I ought to do, Dr. Lapham?' he asked then.

'Yes. One thing above all.'

'I am anxious to get to the bottom of this business, and naturally want to do everything I can.'

'Then go home.'

'To Boston?'

'At once.'

'I can't very well leave him at the mercy of whatever it is out there in the Wood,' Bates protested. 'Besides, he would become suspicious.'

'You contradict yourself, Mr. Bates. It does not matter whether or not he becomes suspicious. I believe, from what you have told me, that your cousin will prove well able to deal with anything that may menace him.'

Bates smiled somewhat boyishly, reached into an inner pocket, and brought out a letter which he laid before my employer. 'Does that sound as if he were able to cope with his problem alone?'

Dr. Lapham read the letter slowly, folded it, and put it back into its envelope. 'As you have indicated, he had undergone some stiffening since he wrote this letter begging you to come.'

To this our visitor agreed. He remained reluctant, however, to alter his plan to return to his cousin's house and remain there until some later date, at which time he might make a less hurried withdrawal.

'I think it highly advisable that you return to Boston now. But if you insist on staying out there, I suggest you make the rest of your stay as short as possible—let us say, three days or so. On your way back to Boston, please stop off here before you take the train.'

To this our visitor finally assented, and got up to go.

'Just a moment, Mr. Bates,' said Dr. Lapham.

My employer crossed the room to a steel cabinet, unlocked it, took something from it, and returned to his desk. He put the object he had taken from the self on his desk before Bates.

'Have you ever seen anything similar to this, Mr. Bates?'

Bates looked at it: a small bas-relief approximately seven inches high, depicting an octopoid monster with a cephalopod head adorned with tentacle-structures, wearing on its back a pair of wings, and showing great, evil claws at its lower extremities. Bates looked at it with horrified fascination, while Dr. Lapham waited patiently.

'It is like—and yet it is not exactly the same as those creatures I saw—or thought I saw out of the study window the other night,' said Bates at last.

'But you have never seen a bas-relief of this nature before?' persisted Dr. Lapham.

'No, never.'

'Nor a drawing?'

Bates shook his head. 'It looks like the things that flew about near the tower—that might have made the clawprints—but it's also like the thing to which my cousin was talking.'

'Ah, you interrupted the scene in that fashion? They were talking?'

'I never consciously thought of it that way—but it must have been that, surely?'

'Some communication seems indicated.'

Bates still kept his eyes fixed on the bas-relief, which, as best I could remember, had an Antarctic origin. 'It is horrible,' he said at last.

'Yes, indeed it is. What is the most horrible aspect of it is the thought that it might have been sculptured from a living model!'

Bates grimaced and shook his head. 'I cannot believe it.'

'We don't know, Mr. Bates. But there are many of us who find it easy to believe the most casual gossip and yet deny the certain evidence of our own senses by convincing ourselves we were experiencing hallucinations.' He shrugged, and picked up the bas-relief, looking at it for a moment before putting it down again. 'Who knows, Mr. Bates? The work is primitive, the concept equally so. But you will want to get back, no doubt, though I still urge Boston.'

Bates shook his head doggedly, shook Dr. Lapham's hand, and took his leave.

Dr. Lapham got up and stretched his muscles a little. I waited for him to make a move to go out for lunch, though it was now mid-afternoon. He made none. Instead, he sat down once more, drew the Bates manuscript over to him, and began to polish his spectacles. He smiled, somewhat grimly, I thought, at my surprise.

'I am afraid you not taking Mr. Bates and his story very seriously, Phillips.'

'Well, it is certainly the most bizarre rigmarole ever adduced to explain those mysterious disappearances.'

'No more bizarre than the circumstances of the disappearances and reappearances themselves. I am not disposed to treat the matter with any levity whatsoever.'

'Surely you're not giving any credence to it?'

He leaned back, holding his spectacles in one hand, and giving me a quieting look. 'You're young, my boy.' Thereupon he launched into a miniature lecture, to all of which I listened with respect and increasing amazement, soon quite oblivious of the pangs of hunger. I must surely be familiar enough with his work, he said, to be aware of the great volume of lore and legend regarding ancient forms of worship, particularly among primitive peoples, and the cult-survivals which have carried through in certain mutations to the present day. There were certain remote areas of Asia, for instance, which had spawned incredible cults, survivals of which turned up contemporaneously in very curious places. He reminded me that Kimmich long ago suggested that the Chimu civilization came from deep within China, though presumably at the time of its origin, China did not exist. At the risk of being banal, he recalled to memory the strange sculptures and carvings of Easter Island and Peru. Worship-patterns have no doubt persisted, sometimes in the old forms, sometimes changed, but never wholly beyond recognition. In Aryan civilization, perhaps the latest to linger with certain definite evidence of survival, were the Druidic rites on the one hand, and the demoniac rites of sorcery and necromancy, particularly in certain parts of France and the

Balkan countries. Did it not occur to me that such worship-patterns bore certain distinct resemblances?

I protested that fundamentally all worship-patterns were similar.

He had reference to aspects over and above the fundamental similarities, which none would argue. He went on to suggest that the idea of beings who would come again was by no means confined to any one group, but there were certain alarming manifestations serving to indicate that there existed in out-of-the-way corners of the earth confirmed worshippers of ancient gods, or god-like beings—god-like in that they were so alien in structure to mankind and indeed to all terrestrial animal life that they attracted worshippers. And by nature, evil.

He took up the bas-relief and held it up. 'Now, you know this has come out of the Antarctic. What would you say it was meant to be?'

'If I had to guess, I would say that it was probably some crude primitive sculptors' concept of what the Indians called the "Wendigo." '

'Not a bad guess, except that there is very little in the lore of the Antarctic to suggest a creature parallel to the Arctic's Wendigo. No, this was found under a portion of a glacier. Its age is very great. As a matter of fact, it would seem to pre-date the Chimu civilization. It is therefore unique in that one factor; it is not unique in others. It may surprise you to know that similar sculptures have cropped up in various ages. We are able to trace some of them all the way back to Cro-Magnon man, and even beyond, into the dawn of what we are fond of calling civilization; we have them from the Middle Ages, we had them from the Ming dynasty, we have them from Russia of Paul I, we have them from Hawaii and the West Indies, we have them from Java of our own day, and we have them from Massachusetts of the Puritans. You may make of that what you will. At the moment it impresses me as singular for quite another reason—because in all likelihood some representation of this figure, possibly in miniature, was what Ambrose Dewart was expected to be carrying when he stopped in Dunwich to find his way to Mrs. Bishop's house and was accosted by the two hamlet derelicts who asked of him whether he had the "sign." '

'Are you suggesting, in a roundabout way, that there actually was a live model for this bas-relief?' I asked.

'I was not standing at the artist's elbow,' he rejoined with exasperating gravity, 'but I am not arrogant enough to deny the possibility.'

'In short, you believe the story this man Bates just told us?'

'I am very much afraid that it is true, within certain limitations.'

'Psychiatric, then!' I retorted.

'Faith comes readily without any evidence whatever, and very hard in the face of evidence that should not be there.' He shook his head. 'I trust you noted the recurrence of the name of one of your own ancestors —the Rev. Ward Phillips?'

'I did.'

'I don't want to seem opportune, but can you look back far enough into your family's history to give me a biographical sketch of the clerical gentleman after his difference of opinion with Alijah Billington?'

'I'm afraid his life was nothing remarkable. He didn't live very long after, and brought a lot of discredit on himself by trying to gather together copies of his book on the curiosa of New England—the *Thaumaturgical Prodigies*—and burn them.'

'That suggests nothing to you in the light of Mr. Bates' manuscript?"

'It is surely a coincidence.'

'I suggest it is more than that. The actions of your ancestor are akin to those of a man who has seen the devil and wishes to recant.'

Dr. Lapham was not much given to levity, and, during the period of my employment by him, I had encountered many strange occurrences and credos. That these manifestations had taken place for the most part in remote, almost inaccessible corners of earth did not preclude the possibility of the occurrence of something similar in our immediate vicinity. In addition, I remembered previous occasions on which Dr. Lapham had seemed to touch upon some monstrous survival-myths, skirting a concept of paralysing dimensions which hinted at something numbingly frightful in its essence.

'Are you suggesting that Alijah Billington corresponded to the devil?' I asked.

'I could answer in both affirmative and negative. From the known evidence—as devil's advocate, certainly. Alijah Billington was quite clearly a man well ahead of his time, more intelligent than most men of his generation, and capable of recognizing the extremities of danger when he encountered them. He practised rites and ceremonies which undoubtedly harked back to the beginnings of mankind, but he knew how to escape the consequences. So it would seem. I believe that a thorough study of these documents and this manuscript would be advisable. I am going to lose no time.'

'I think you may be attaching too much importance to this rigmarole.'

He shook his head. 'The scientific attitude of labelling many things we do not immediately understand, or which do not fit into some already-conceived scientific credo, as "coincidence," "hallucination," or something similar is deplorable. In regard to the things which have taken place in Billington's Wood and in the surrounding terrain, notably Dunwich, I would say it is beyond the bounds of credibility that it can be passed off as coincidence that, each time there is activity in Billington's Wood, there are strange disappearances in Dunwich and that country. We need not take heed of Mr. Bates' manuscript at all, except in so far as he has quoted contemporaneous accounts, the originals of which we can look up for ourselves without trouble if we choose to disregard what Bates has written. These phenomena have recurred at least three times in generations more than two hundred years apart. I have no doubt that on their initial occurrence they were laid to sorcery, and there is every likelihood that some luckless person or persons suffered and died for events which were brought about completely beyond his or their ken. The witch-hunting and witch-burning days were not then too distant, and hysterics and the conniving we have always with us. In Alijah's time some glimmer of the truth in the matter must have penetrated to the Rev. Ward Phillips and the reviewer, John Druven, and they were actually led to visit Billington, whereupon something happened to them—Druven disappeared and followed the customary course of the victims out of Dunwich, the Rev. Ward Phillips could not remember anything of his visit to Billington save that it had been made, and subsequently tried to destroy his book, which—mark this—contained references to events of a somewhat similar nature which had taken place decades before. In our own time, we find our Mr. Bates encountering the inexplicable hostility of Ambrose Dewart, after his cousin has sent for him in a rather frantic letter imploring his assistance. There is a certain pattern in all this.'

I granted that without argument.

'I know there are those who will suggest that the house itself is evil, and Bates' manuscript in places does so, too, and will propound a theory of psychic residue, but I think it is far more than that—far, far more—something incredibly more hideous and malign which is well beyond the present known events in its significance.'

The profound gravity of Dr. Lapham's demeanour made it impossible to doubt for a moment the importance he attached to the Bates manuscript. Clearly he meant to follow it up, and the way in which he now began to move around, gathering various volumes from his reference shelves, suggested that he was indeed, as he had said, losing no time. He paused to suggest that I go out to lunch, and on the way deliver a note to Dr. Armitage Harper, which he immediately set about to write. He seemed now tremendously exhilarated and extremely zestful, writing rapidly and in his usual flowing hand, folding his note expertly, and sealing it into an envelope to hand to me with the warning to make my lunch a heavy one for 'We may be here through the dinner hour.'

On my return from lunch three-quarters of an hour later, I found Dr. Lapham surrounded by books and papers, among them a large, sealed book which I recognized as the property of the Library of Miskatonic University, doubtless sent over at Dr. Lapham's request. The pages of the Bates manuscript had been separated, and several of them were marked.

'Can I help?'

'At the moment only by keeping an open mind, Phillips. Sit down.' He got up and strode across to a window, from which he could look down to the compound before the Miskatonic University Library, and to the great dog chained there as if on guard. 'I often think,' he said over his shoulder, 'how fortunate most men are in their inability to correlate all the knowledge at their disposal. Bates, I believe, illustrates the point very well. He has recorded what seems to be dissociated knowledge, he constantly skirts a terrifying reality, he seldom makes any genuine attempt to face it; he is hampered by the superficial, by vestigial superstitions and credos which have no reality apart from the expected conventional behaviour- and belief-patterns of the average human being. If the common man were even to suspect the cosmic grandeur of the universe, if he were to have a glimpse of the awesome depths of outer space, he would very likely either go mad or reject such knowledge in preference to superstition. It is so with other things. Bates has set down a series of events ranging over two centuries, somewhat more, and he has every opportunity to solve the mystery of

Billington's Wood, but he fails to do so. He sets forth the events, as if they were pieces of a jig-saw; he draws certain preliminary conclusions—for instance, that his ancestor, Alijah Billington, was engaged in some very strange and possibly illegal practices, which were inevitably accompanied by stranger disappearances in the vicinity—but he goes no farther. He actually sees and hears certain phenomena, and then proceeds to argue against his own senses; in short, he represents pretty much the average mind—face to face with manifestations which are not "in the books," so to speak, he finds it both simpler and more intelligent to take issue with his senses. He writes about "imagination" and "hallucination"; yet he is honest enough to concede that his reactions are "normal" enough to give the lie to his retreating arguments. In the end, though it is true he does not seem to have the final key with which to unlock the puzzle, he lacks the courage to fit what pieces he has together and obtain a solution of wider significance than the outlines at which he barely hints. So he takes flight, in effect, and lays the problem before Dr. Harper, from whom it comes to me.'

I asked whether he proceeded on the assumption that the Bates manuscript was a scrupulously factual account.

'I think little alternative is offered. It is either factual or it is not. If we deny its factuality, then we are in the position of denying known events which have been recorded, witnessed, and have gone into history. If we accept only those known facts, we are then likely to explain every other event it chronicles as a manifestation of "chance" or "coincidence," quite regardless of the fact that the mathematical average of such a series of chances and coincidences is vastly beyond acceptance by any scientific procedure. It seems to me therefore that we have actually no alternative. Bates' manuscript sets forth a series of events which correlate with the known history of the place and inhabitants of his narrative. If, finally, you want to suggest that certain parts of Bates' manuscript are imaginary events, then you must feel ready to explain from what source does his extraterrestrial imagination arise—for his descriptions are lucid, almost scholarly, and include such detail as to suggest that he did actually see something of the kind he describes, and there is nothing in the known history of man or the mutations of man to account for certain of those details. Even if, as you might futher suggest, these so carefully described creatures were the product of a nightmare, you must still adduce reason to people his nightmares with such beings, for the moment you postulate that any human being's dreams or nightmares can be inhabited by creatures wholly alien to all his actual experience in life and also all his psychic existence, your postulate is as contrary to scientific fact as are the creatures themselves. It suits our purpose only if the manuscript is accepted as a factual account; we must go on from there, and if we are in error, time will surely tell.'

He returned to his desk and sat down. 'You will remember reading during your first year here about certain curious rites performed by the natives on Ponape, in the Caroline Islands, in worship of a deity of the seas, a Water-Being, who was at first thought to be the familiar fish-god, Dagon, but at the suggestion of which the natives were agreed in declaring that He was greater than Dagon, that Dagon and his Deep Ones served Him. Such cult-survivals are common enough, and don't often come to public notice, but this one was publicized because of certain adjunctive discoveries—the queer mutations present on the bodies of certain of the natives killed in a shipwreck just off the coast—the presence of primal gills, for instance of vestigial tentacles arising from the torso, and in one case, of scaly eyes in an area of squamous skin near the navel of one of the victims, all of whom were known to have belonged to the Sea-God cult. The one assertion of these islanders which comes back rather vividly to my mind is the statement that their god came out of the stars. Now, you know that there is a marked resemblance among the religious beliefs and myth-patterns of the Atlanteans, the Mayans, the Druids, and others, and we are constantly finding basic similarities, particularly connecting the seas and the skies, as for instance, in the god Quetzalcoatl, who bears parallelisms to the Hellenic Atlas, in that he supposedly came from some place in the Atlantic Ocean to bear the world on his shoulders. Not only in religion, but in pure legend also, as for instance, in the extension of god-credos to human giants, whose origin is supposedly also the sea—the western seas, to be precise, as did the Greek Titans, the island giants of Spanish tales, and the Cornwall giants of sunken Lyonesse. I mention this to point the curious linkage to tradition that goes back to primal times, when it was believed that great beings resided in the depths of the sea, a belief which clearly gave rise to that secondary belief about the origin of giants. We ought not to be surprised at the evidence of such cult-survivals as that on Ponape, since there is every precedent for it; but we are surprised and confounded by physical mutations which have occurred there, and which are subsequently explained by dark hints—no facts, of course—that there has been carnal traffic between certain sea-dwellers and some of the natives of the Carolines. This, if true, would indeed account for the mutations. But science, lacking actual positive evidence of the existence of any such sea-dwellers, simply denies that it is true; the mutations are dismissed as "negative" evidence, and hence not admissible, and an elaborate explanation is concocted to show that primitive outcroppings are not unknown, the natives are ticketed as "throwbacks," as "atavistic" curiosities, and the incident duly filed away. If you or I or anyone else once decides to lay these incidents end to end, he will find that they can encircle the globe several times, and not only that, they will present certain disturbing similarities, in effect supporting one another and emphasizing repetitive aspects of those curious happenings. No one, however, is quite willing to undertake an impartial study of those isolated phenomena because, as in the case of Mr. Bates, there does exist a certain very real and quite human fear of what one may find. Better not to disturb the pattern of existence, for fear of what may lie just beyond, in an extension of time or space with which none of us is prepared to cope.'

I remembered the account of the Ponape islanders and said so. I did not quite follow my employer, however, in his inference that this concerned the Bates manuscript, even remotely, though I felt certain that there was purpose in Dr. Lapham's recalling the incident to my memory.

He went on with meticulous detail to explain.

In a great many of the scattered phenomena presented to anthropolgists, among others, there existed a certain pattern common to all. It was a mythology of belief in primal inhabitation of earth by another race of beings who, because of certain dark practices, lost their foothold on earth and were expelled by 'Elder Gods,' who sealed them away in time and space—since they were not subject to the laws of time and space as were we mere mortal men and were in addition mobile in other dimensions. These other beings, despite being expelled and sealed away by fearful and hated seals, continue to live on 'outside' and are frequently manifest in attempts to regain their control over and possession of earth and the 'inferior' beings who now inhabit it—inferior, presumably, because of their subjectivity to lesser laws which do not affect the expelled beings who were known by various names, most common among them being the 'Great Old Ones,' and who were served by many primitive peoples—such as the Ponape Islanders, as an instance. Moreover, these 'Great Old Ones' are malevolent, and it should be recognized that the barriers which stand between mankind and the paralysing horror which they represent are purely arbitrary and wholly inadequate.

'But this might have been evolved from the Bates

manuscript and the documents accompanying it!' I protested.

'Yet it was not. It existed decades before the Bates manuscript came into existence.'

'Bates must have discovered its lore.'

He was unperturbed, but no whit less grave. 'Even if he did, that does not explain the undisputable fact that a horrible and exceedingly rare book was written about the Great Old Ones and traffic with them in about the year A.D. 730 at Damascus by an Arab poet named Abdul Alhazred, who was commonly thought to be mad, and who titled his book *Al Azif,* though it is now more widely known in certain secret circles by its Greek title of *Necronomicon.* I suggest that if this legend and lore has been chronicled as fact centuries ago, and certain non-human phenomena arise in our own day which would seem to corroborate certain aspects of the Arab's writings, it is decidedly unscientific to lay these phenomena to the imagination or machination of a human being, particularly one who gives no evidence of foreknowledge in these matters.'

'Very well. Go on.'

The Great Old Ones, he continued, had some correspondence to the elements—as of earth, water, air, fire—these were likewise their media, over and above a certain interdependence and their supramundane faculties which rendered them insensible to the effects of time and space, so that they represented an ever-present menace to mankind and indeed to all the creatures on earth, to which their incessant strivings to come through again were aided by their primitive worshippers and followers, who were for the most part of inferior physical or mental stock, and in some cases, as was shown by the Ponape Islanders, actual physiological mutations, who effected certain 'openings' through which the Great Old Ones and their extraterrestrial minions might enter, or might be 'called,' wherever in space or time they might be, by certain rites, which were in part at least chronicled by the Arab,

Abdul Alhazred, and by various lesser writers who followed him and left a parallel lore of their own, stemming from the same source, but augmented by various data which had come into being since the Arab's time.

Here he paused and gazed intently at me. 'Do you follow me, Phillips?'

I assured him that I did.

'Very well. Now, these Great Old Ones, as I have said, have been given various names. There were certain inferior ones, who are in numerical superiority. These are not quite as free as the remaining few, and many of them are subject to many of the same laws which govern mankind. The first among them is Cthulhu, who lies supposedly "dead but dreaming" in the unknown sunken city of R'lyeh, which some writers have thought to be in Atlantis, some in Mu, and some few in the sea not far off the coast of Massachusetts. Second among them is Hastur, sometimes called Him Who Is Not To Be Named and Hastur the Unspeakable, who supposedly resides in Hali in the Hyades. Third is Shub-Niggurath, a horrible travesty on a god or goddess of fertility. Next comes one who is described as the "Messenger of the Gods"—Nyarlathotep—and particularly of the most powerful extension of the Great Old Ones, the noxious Yog-Sothoth, who shares the dominion of Azathoth, the blind and idiot chaos at the centre of infinity. I see by the expression of your eyes that you are beginning to recognize some of these names.'

'Yes, of course; they were in the manuscript.'

'And likewise in the documents. It should give you pause to learn that Nyarlathotep is often accompanied in his faceless manifestations by creatures described as "idiot flute-players."'

'What Bates saw!'

'Yes.'

'But then—what were those others?'

'That we can only conjecture. But if Nyarlathotep

is always accompanied by the idiot flute-players, presumably one of those manifestations was he. The Great Old Ones have to some degree the ability to appear in mutations, though each presumably has his own identity and shape. Abdul Alhazred describes him as "faceless," while Ludvig Prinn, in his *De Vermis Mysteriis,* has it the Nyarlathotep was the "all-seeing eye," and Von Junzt, writing in *Unaussprechlichen Kulten,* says he was, in common with another of the Great Old Ones— which is presumably Cthulhu—"adorned with tentacles." These various descriptions certainly cover the manifestations that Bates saw as an "excrescence" or "extension." '

I was astonished at the lore which was apparently available in connection with these primitive or primal cults and religions. I had never before heard my employer speak of these books, and certainly he did not own them. Where then had he learned of them?

'Why, they are seldom seen. This book'—he tapped the strange book I had seen on my return from lunch —'is the most famous of them, and I must return it tonight. It is the Latin version of Olaus Wormius of the *Necronomicon,* printed in Spain in the seventeenth century. This, in point of fact, is the "Book" referred to in the Bates manuscript and the documents, and it was this book from which pages and paragraphs were copied by correspondents of Alijah Billington's in various places of the world—for there are copies in whole or in part only at the Widener, at the British Museum, the Universities of Buenos Aires and Lima, the Bibliotheque Nationale of Paris, and our own Miskatonic. Some say that a hidden copy exists in Cairo, and another in the Vatican Library in Rome; some also believe that portions of this book, copied laboriously exist in various private hands, and this has to some extent been substantiated in what Bates found in his cousin's library, which had been Alijah Billington's. If Billington managed it, then others could manage it as well.'

He got up and took a bottle of old wine from a

cupboard and poured himself a glass to sip apprecia-
tively. He stood for a while at the window once more,
while outside darkness began to gather, and the evening noises of the somewhat provincial city of Arkham
rose. Then he turned and came back again.

'That should suffice for the background,' he said.

'Do you expect me to believe it?' I asked.

'Not at all; of course not. But suppose we accept it
as a provisional hypothesis and pass on to an examination of the Billington mystery itself.'

I agreed.

'Very well, then. Let us start with Alijah Billington
—that, it appears, is where both Dewart and Bates
began. I think we can agree without cavil that Alijah
Billington was engaged in some kind of nefarious practice which may or may not have been akin to sorcery,
which I suspect the Rev. Ward Phillips and John
Druven thought it was. We have certain evidence connecting Alijah's activity to the Wood—specifically, to
the peculiar stone tower in the Wood, and we know that
it was done at night—"after the hour at which the
supper is served," according to Alijah's son, Laban.
Into this business, whatever it was, the Indian Quamis
was likewise initiated, though apparently in a more
servile capacity. The Indian once mentions in awed
tones in the boy's hearing a name which is that of
Nyarlathotep. At the same time, we have the evidence
of the Bishop letters to indicate that Jonathan Bishop
of Dunwich was engaged in similar practices. These
letters are fairly clear on the subject. Jonathan had
learned enough to call something out of the sky, but
not enough to close the opening against others, or to
protect himself. The inference is plain that whatever
it was came in answer to such a summons had some
use for human beings, and the suggestion is, also quite
clearly, that that use was as food of some kind. If we
can accept that, we can thus account for the multiple
disappearances, no one of which was ever solved.'

'But how then account for the reappearances of the

bodies?' I interjected. 'There was never any evidence adduced to show where they had been.'

'Nor would there be—if they were, as I suspect they were—in another dimension. The implication is dreadfully and frighteningly clear—whatever came in answer to the call was not always the same—you will remember the sense of the letters and the instructions about raising various named beings—and it came out of another dimension, and retreated into that dimension again, not impossibly without carrying back an inferior creature —in short, a human being—upon which to feed, whether for life force or blood or something more obscure, we cannot conjecture. It was for that purpose, as well as to shut his mouth, that John Druven was doubtless drugged and brought back to Billington's house and offered as a sacrifice in exactly the same vengeful manner employed by Jonathan Bishop against the prying Wilbur Corey.'

'Granting all that—there is a certain evidence of contradiction in the known facts,' I said.

'Ah, I hoped you would see it. Yes, it is there. It demands to be seen and recognized, and that it was not recognized by Bates was a serious flaw in his reasoning. Let me advance an hypothesis. Alijah Billington, by some means we know not of, stumbles upon certain of the lore of the Great Old Ones on the ancestral property. He investigates, continues to instruct himself, and eventually manages to put to its intended use the circle of stones and the tower on the island in the tributary to the Miskatonic—the river Dewart so strangely named the Misquamacus, out of a memory not his own. Careful as he is, however, he cannot prevent occasional raids upon the Dunwich inhabitants. Perhaps he comforts and excuses himself with the thought that it is Bishop's work which is responsible. He carefully assimilates portions of the *Necronomicon,* as we have seen, from all over the world, but at the same time he is becoming somewhat nervous about the vastness and immensity of the extraterrestrial infinity into which he has reached. His outburst against Druven's review of the Rev. Ward Phillips' book is symptomatic of two things—he has began to suspect that his hand is not entirely his own, and he has begun to struggle against a compulsion that is not solely his own. The direct attack on and death of Druvan brings matters to a climax. Billington takes his leave of Quamis, and, by the use of knowledge gained from the *Necronomicon,* he seals the "opening" he has made, even as he has sealed the Bishop opening after Bishop's disappearance, and sets out for England, to resume his own identity away from the sinister psychic forces in operation in the Wood.'

'That sounds logical.'

'Now, in the light of that hypothesis, let us look at the instructions Alijah Billington handed down concerning the Massachusetts estate.' He selected a sheet of paper in Bates' hand, and propped it up before him, turning on the green-shaded light over his desk. 'Here we are. First of all, he adjures "all who come after" that the property should be kept in the family, and then he imparts a set of rules, deliberately obscure, though he somewhat obliquely admits that their "sense shall be found within such books as have been left in the house known as Billington's house." He begins with this one: "He is not to cause the water to cease flowing about the island of the tower, nor to molest the tower in any way, nor to entreat of the stones." The water ceased to flow of itself, and so far as we know, no evil consequences impended. By molestation of the tower, Alijah clearly meant that it was not to be disturbed in such a way as to *restore* the opening he had closed. As is evident, the opening he had closed was the roof of the tower; he had closed it with a stone bearing a mark which, though I have not seen it, must and can only be the *Elder Sign,* the mark of those Elder Gods whose strength against the Great Old Ones is absolute, the mark Great Old Ones fear and hate. Dewart molested this in precisely the way Alijah hoped it would not be disturbed. Finally, the entreaty to which reference is made can refer only to a formula or formulae to be recited in order to effect the primary stage of contact with the forces beyond the threshold.

'He goes on to say: "He is not to open the door which leads to strange time and place, nor to invite Him Who lurks at the threshold, nor to call out to the hills." The first part only emphasizes again the adjuration initially made about the stone tower. The second refers for the first time to a very definite Being, a lurker at the threshold, whose identity we do not know—he may be Nyarlathotep, he may be Yog-Sothoth, he may be another. And the third must have reference to a secondary stage of the rites attendant upon a manifestation of *those from outside,* quite possibly to the sacrifice.

'The third adjuration is again in the nature of a warning: "He is not to disturb the frogs, particularly the bull-frogs of the marshland between the tower and the house, nor the fireflies, nor the birds known as whip-poor-wills, lest he abandon his locks and his guards.' Bates did begin to guess at the meaning of this adjuration—which is meant simply to say that the named creatures have shown a peculiar sensitivity to the presence of *those from outside,* and, by the tempo of their cries and lights, give warning and thus allow preparation. Any step taken against them, then, is presumably a step against self-interest.

'In the fourth, the window is mentioned for the first time. "He is not to touch upon the window, seeking to change it in any way." Why not? From everything Bates has put down, there is a malignant quality about the window. If his adjurations are protective, why not then destroy the window, since he is cognizant of its evil? I think it is simply because the window changed must be more dangerous than the window as it is.'

'I don't follow there,' I interrupted.

'Does nothing of Bates' narrative suggest anything to you?'

'The window is strange, the glass different—it was designed that way, obviously.'

'I suggest the window is not a window at all, but a lens or prism or mirror reflecting vision from another dimension or dimensions—in short, from time or space. It may also be designed to reflect obscure rays, not of vision, but operating on vestigial and forgotten extra senses, and its construction may not have been the work of human hands at all. It enabled Bates on two occasions to see beyond the natural landscape which lies beyond that window.'

'Accepting that tentatively, let us go on to the last adjuration.'

'The last is simply a reaffirmation of everything essential that has gone before, and is clear enough in the light of what the previous instructions portend. "He is not to sell or otherwise make disposition of the property without inserting a clause to hold that the island and the tower are in no wise disturbed, nor the window be alter'd except it be destroy'd." The suggestion is here again that the window is somehow capable of wielding an evil influence, and that, in turn, suggests that in some fashion unknown even to Alijah, it is a further opening —if not for the physical entry of *those from outside,* for their perceptions, and thus also for their suggestions, or influence. I think that the most likely explanation for a very patent reason—it is this: in every avenue of information open to us, it is manifest that some *influence* is at work in the house as well as the Wood. Alijah is impelled to study and experiment. Bates tells us that when Dewart took the house, he was drawn to the window, to examine it, to look out of it; and when he went into the tower in the Wood, he felt a compulsion to dislodge the block set into the roof. Bates himself sets down his reaction to the house after his first curious experience with his cousin, which he mistakenly labels "schizophrenic." I have it here; let me read it to you. "And suddenly, as I stood there, feeling the freshness of the wind against my body, I was conscious with a rapidly mounting oppression, with a crushing sense of despair, of a horrible foulness, of a black, blasting evil of and around this woods-girt house, a cloying, infiltrating loathsomeness of the nethermost abysses of the human soul. . . . The apprehension of evil, of terror and loathing, settled like a cloud in the room; I felt it pour from the walls like invisible fog." In addition to this, Bates, too, is drawn to the window. And finally, being newer in the house, he is able to observe from a comparatively unbiased perspective the influence at work in his cousin. He diagnoses it correctly as some kind of inner "struggle"; he labels it, incorrectly, as "schizophrenia," which it is not.'

'Aren't you going out of bounds in being so positive? After all, there appears to be some evidence of split-personality.'

'No, no, none whatsoever. That is the danger of knowing too little about a subject. None of the symptoms is present, save only the superficial conflict between moods. Ambrose Dewart is quite clearly at first a rather amiable soul, a pottering gentleman, a country squire lazily in search of something to occupy his time. Then he becomes aware of something—he knows not what—and he grows uneasy. Finally he sends for his cousin. Bates finds a further change; now Dewart is uneasy with him, and presently he becomes definitely hostile. There are brief returnings to his earlier, more natural state, and a prolonged return in the Boston sojourn during the past winter. But almost at once on the return to the house in the Wood last month the previous hostility became manifest again, and presently, as Bates does not himself seem to perceive as well as he might, this gives way to a guarded awareness. The effect on Bates is simply that one time he feels welcome, one time he does not, quite the opposite. He recognizes a conflict in his cousin, and in terms of psychiatry, of which he knows no more than you, Phillips, this suggests schizophrenia.'

'You suggest influence, then—from *outside*. Of what nature?'

'Why, I think that is fairly evident. The influence is that of a directing intelligence. It is, specifically, the same influence which went to work on Alijah but was defeated by him.'

'One of the Great Old Ones, then?'

'No, that is not shown.'

'Indicated, then.'

'No, not even indicated. The manifest suggestion is the influence of an agent of the Great Old Ones. If you will examine the Bates manuscript carefully, you will find that the suggestions, the influences implanted are of an essentially human nature. I postulate that if the Great Old Ones themselves were activating the influence at work in Billington House, the suggestions implanted would, at least on occasion, be essentially non-human. There is nothing to show that they are. If the impression conveyed to Bates of the foulness and loathsomeness and evil about the house and Wood had been conveyed by something alien, it is probable that his reaction would not have been so fundamentally human; no, he was enveloped on that occasion by a reaction which was human with almost a calculated humanity.'

I pondered this. If Dr. Lapham's theory were sound —and indeed it seemed so—there seemed to be a manifest flaw in it; he had suggested that the 'influence' at work on Dewart and Bates had also worked on Alijah Billington. If that 'influence' were, as he had postulated, of human origin, it would have more than spanned a century. Choosing my words carefully, I pointed out this objection.

'Yes, I accept it. I find it not incompatible. You will bear in mind that the influence is extra-terrestrial in origin. It is also extra-dimensional, and therefore, human or not, no more subject to the laws of physical earth than the Great Old Ones. In short, if the influence is human, as I postulate it is, then it, too, exists in the time and space conterminous with us, and yet not similar. It shares the ability to exist in such dimensions without experiencing the limitations time and space exercise upon any person or persons who occupy Billington House. It exists in those dimensions exactly as those poor unfortunates did who were victims of the beings called by Bishop and Billington and Dewart before they were dropped back into our dimension.'

'Dewart!'

'Yes, he, too.'

'You suggest that he is responsible for those strange disappearances recently from Dunwich?' I asked in astonishment.

He shook his head somewhat pityingly. 'No, I do not *suggest* it; I advance it as *manifest fact*—unless you now want to return to the objectionable grounds of coincidence.'

'Not at all.'

'Very well, then. Consider it. Billington goes off to his circle of stones and his stone tower and opens the "door." Noises are heard in the woods by persons completely dissociated from Billington, as well as by his son, Laban, who writes about them in his daybook. These phenomena are always followed by a) a disappearance; b) a reappearance under certain strange, but repetitive, conditions weeks or months later—both unsolved. Jonathan Bishop writes in his letters that he went to his circle of stones and "call'd It to yᵉ hill, and contain'd It in yᵉ circle, but onlie with yᵉ greatest difficultie and hardship, so that 'twould but seem it is not likelie that yᵉ circle is potent enough to contain such as These for long." Thereafter, likewise, strange disappearances, and equally strange reappearances in circumstances paralleling those following Billington's activities. These things of a century and more ago are repeated in our own time. Ambrose Dewart walks in his sleep to the tower; in his dreams he is conscious of something incredibly awesome and terrible; he is possessed by that external influence, but he is not aware of it. Surely you do not expect any impartial observer, in the light of these facts, to believe that, after Dewart's trip to the stone tower, at which he subsequently finds what appears to be a splashing of blood, the disappearances and reappearances which follow are only "coincidence"?'

I conceded that an explanation involving coincidence to explain such a series of parallel events was fully as fantastic as the explanation Dr. Lapham himself offered. I was troubled and deeply disturbed, because Dr. Seneca Lapham was a scholar of great breadth and a singular store of knowledge, and his espousal of something thus far foreign to absolute knowledge had the impact of a profound shock on one whose respect for him was unbounded. Clearly, to Dr. Lapham, the hypotheses he put forward were based on more than conjecture, and this involved a belief almost beyond credibility. Yet it was manifest that my employer had no doubt whatsoever, secure in a greater knowledge of his subject and its background.

'I observe you are involved within your own thoughts. Let us just turn this over in our minds tonight, and return to it tomorrow or later. I want you to read some of the passages I have marked in these books, though you will have to glance at the *Necronomicon* here and now, so that I can return it to the Library tonight.'

I turned at once to the ancient book in which Dr. Lapham had marked two curious passages, which I translated slowly as I read. They were passages hinting of hideous outsiders constantly lying in wait; indeed, the Arab author referred to them as 'the Liers-in-Wait,' and he gave them names. A long paragraph in the midst of the first passage struck me with especial force.

'Ubbo-Sathla is that unforgotten source whence came those daring to oppose the Elder Gods who ruled from Betelgueze; the Great Old Ones who fought against the Elder Gods; and these Old Ones were instructed by Azathoth, who is the blind, idiot god, and by Yog-

Sothoth, who is the All-in-One and One-in-All, and upon whom are no strictures of time or space, and whose aspects on earth are 'Umr At-Tawil and the Ancient Ones. The Great Old Ones dream forever of that coming time when they shall once more rule Earth and all that Universe of which it is part. . . . Great Cthulhu shall rise from R'lyeh; Hastur, who is Him Who Is Not To Be Named, shall come again from the dark star which is near Aldebaran in the Hyades; Nyarlathotep shall howl forever in darkness where he abideth; Shub-Niggurath, who is the Black Goat With a Thousand Young, shall spawn and spawn again, and shall have dominion over all wood nymphs, satyrs, leprechauns, and the Little People; Lloigor, Zhar, and Ithaqua shall ride the spaces among the stars and shall ennoble those who are their followers, who are the Tcho-Tcho; Cthugha shall encompass his dominion from Fomalhaut; Tsathoggua shall come from N'kai. . . . They wait forever at the Gates, for the time draws near, the hour is soon at hand, while the Elder Gods sleep, dreaming, unknowing there are those who know the spells put upon the Great Old Ones by the Elder Gods, and shall learn how to break them, as already they can command the followers waiting beyond the doors from Outside.'

The second passage occurred somewhat later, and was equally potent:

'Armor against witches and daemons, against the Deep Ones, the Dholes, the Voormis, the Tcho-Tcho, the Abominable Mi-Go, the Shoggoths, the Ghasts, the Valusians and all such peoples and beings who serve the Great Old Ones and their Spawn lies within the five-pointed star carven of grey stone from ancient Mnar, which is less strong against the Great Old Ones themselves. The possessor of the stone shall find himself able to command all beings which creep, swim, crawl, walk, or fly even to the source from which there is no returning. In Yhe as in great R'lyeh, in Y'ha-nthlei as in Yoth, in Yuggoth as in Zothique, in N'kai

169

as in K'n-yan, in Kadath in the Cold Waste as at the Lake of Hali, in Carcosa as in Ib, it shall have power; yet, even as stars wane and grow cold, even as suns die and the spaces between stars grow more wide, so wanes the power of all things—of the five-pointed star-stone as of the spells put upon the Great Old Ones by the benign Elder Gods, and there cometh a time as once was a time, when it shall be shown that

That is not dead which can eternal lie.
And with strange eons even death may die.'

I took the other books and certain photostat copies of manuscript books which were forbidden egress from the Miskatonic Library home with me, and throughout most of that night I dipped into strange and terrible pages. I read in the *Pnakotic Manuscript,* in the *Celaeno Fragments,* in Professor Shewsbury's *An Investigation into the Myth-Patterns of Latter-day Primitives with Especial Reference to the R'lyeh Text,* in the *R'lyeh Text* itself, in Comte d'Erlette's *Cultes des Goules,* the *Libor Ivonis,* the *Unaussprechlichen Kulten* of Von Junzt, the *De Vermis Mysteriis* of Ludwig Prinn, the *Book of Dzyan,* the *Dhol Chants,* and the *Seven Cryptical Books of Hsan.* I read of terrible and blasphemous cults of ancient, pre-human eras which had survived in certain unmentionable forms to our own day in remote corners of the earth; I pored over cryptic accounts of obscure, pre-human languages which bore such names as *Aklo, Naacal, Tsatho-yo* and *Chian;* I came upon horrible hints of abysmally evil rites and 'games,' such as the *Mao* and the *Lloyathic;* I found repeated mention of placenames of incredible antiquity—of the Vale of Pnath, or Ulthar, of N'gai and Ngranek, of Ooth-Nargai and Sarnath-the-Doomed, of Throk and Inganok, of Kythamil and Lemuria, of Hatheg-Kla and Chorazin, of Carcosa and Yaddith, of Lomar and Yian-Ho; and I came upon other Beings, whose names were set forth in the nightmare of unbelievably, shuddersome horror, made all the more terrible by accompanying accounts of certain strange and incredible terrestrial happenings, *explicable only in the light of this hellish lore*—I found strange names and familiar ones, awful descriptions and mere hints of terror unimaginable in accounts of Yig, the terrible snake-god, of Atlach-Nacha of the spider-shape, of Gnoph-Hek, the 'hairy thing' otherwise known as Rhan-Tegoth, of Chaugnar Faugn, the vampiric 'feeder,' of the hell-hounds of Tindalos, which prowl the angles of time, and again and again of the monstrous Yog-Sothoth, the 'All-in-One and One-in-All,' whose deceptive disguise is as a congeries of iridescent globes concealing the primal horror beneath. I read such things as mortal man is not meant to know, such things as would blast the sanity of the imaginative reader, such things as are best destroyed, for the knowledge of them may be as grave a danger to mankind as the fearful consequences of a return to terrestrial dominion of those Great Old Ones who were exiled forever from the star-kingdom of Betelgueze by the Elder Gods whose rule these evil ones had defied.

I read throughout most of that night, and for the remainder of it lay awake, turning over and over in mind the nauseatingly fearful data I had read, myself afraid to sleep, lest in dream I encounter the subconsciously visualized beings of the grotesque and horrible mythology which I had encountered within the past hours not alone in these books, but also in the persuasive instructions of Dr. Seneca Lapham, whose anthropological knowledge few of his contemporaries could equal, and fewer still exceed. Moreover, I was too stirred to sleep, for the concepts revealed to me in the pages of these rare and frightening volumes were so vast and so all-inclusive in the terror and horror they held out for mankind that my sole conscious endeavour was expended in the direction of rationalizing myself once again into a normal state of mind.

I returned to Dr. Lapham's office earlier than usual the next morning, but my employer was there before me. He had evidently been working for a long time, for his desk was covered with sheets of paper upon which he had scrawled formulae, graphs, charts, and diagrams of an utterly outré nature.

'Ah, you have read them,' he said, as I put the books down at one corner of his desk.

'All night,' I replied.

'I, too—night after night, when first I discovered them.'

'If these things are only in the smallest part true, then we shall have to revise all our concepts of time and space—and even, to some extent, of our own beginnings.'

He nodded imperturbably. 'Every scientist knows that most of our knowledge is based upon certain fundamental credos which, faced with a non-terrestrial intelligence, are not provable. Perhaps we shall need ultimately to make certain changes in our credos. What we are faced with in what is commonly called "the Unknown" is still a matter of conjecture, despite these and other books. But I think we cannot doubt but that *something* exists *outside,* and this myth-pattern allows of forces of good as well as forces of evil, precisely as do certain other patterns I need not emphasize in too much detail, since you know them—the Christian, the Buddhist, the Mohammedan, the Confucian, the Shinto—in fact, commonly, *all* known religion-patterns. The reason I say specifically in regard to this particular myth-pattern that we must admit of the existence of something alien outside is simply that, as you will have seen, only by its acceptance at least in large part can we explain not only the strange and terrible accounts chronicled in the adjunctive data in these books, but also a very large, though usually suppressed, body of occurrences antipodally contradictory to the total scientific knowledge of mankind, which occur daily in all parts of the world, some of which have been collected and chronicled in two remarkable books by a comparative unknown named Charles Fort—*The*

Book of the Damned and *New Lands*—I commend them to your attention.

'Consider a few facts, and I say "facts" advisedly, allowing for the well-known unreliability of human observers. The fall of stones from the sky at Buschof, Pillitsfer, Nerft, and Dolgovdi in Russia in a period from 1863 into 1864. Of no known terrestrial substance, described as "grey, with an occasional flecking of brown." The stone from Mnar to which frequent reference is made, I emphasize, is likewise described as a "grey stone." Similarly, the Rowley ragstones of a few years before in Birmingham, England and subsequently at Wolverhampton, these being black outside, but grey within.

'Again, the "globular lights" of H.M.S. *Caroline*, reported in 1893, as seen between the ship and a mountain off the China sea. The lights were described as "globular"; they were seen in the heavens, at not quite the height of the mountain, and well away from it; they moved in mass, on occasion, and sometimes irregularly strung out. They were moving northward, and were seen for two hours or thereabouts. They were seen the following night again, on two nights, then—the twenty-fourth and twenty-fifth of February, at both times an hour or so before midnight. They cast a reflection, and in the telescope were thought to be roseate in colour. On the second night, as on the first, their movement appeared to be equal to that of the *Caroline*. On this night the phenomenon lasted seven hours. A similar phenomenon reported seen by the captain of H.M.S. *Leander*, who, however, asserted that the lights moved straight up into the sky and vanished. Eleven years later to the day, February twenty-fourth, the crew of the U.S.S. *Supply* saw three objects of different sizes, but all "globular," likewise moving upward in "unison," and apparently not susceptible to "forces of this earth and of the air." In the meantime, a similar globular light was seen by travellers in a train near Trenton, Missouri, and reported to the *Monthly*

Weather Review for August, 1898, by a railroad postal clerk, the light appearing during a rain, and moving steadily along with the train in a northward direction, despite a violent east wind, moving at various speeds and heights, until the approach to a small village in Iowa, where it disappeared. In 1925, during an exceptionally hot August, a pair of young men walking across a bridge over the Wisconsin River in the village of Sac Prairie, saw in the evening sky, at about ten o'clock, a singular band of light crossing the southern horizon from a point in the east passing through the star Antares to a point in the west passing near Arcturus, and being traversed by a "ball of black light, sometimes round, sometimes ovoid, sometimes lozengelike in a shape," the band remaining until this distant object had traversed its entire length from the southeast into the northwest, after which it faded and vanished. Does all that suggest anything?'

My throat had gone dry with the impact of growing conviction. 'Only that one of the Great Old Ones presents a superficial appearance as a "congeries of iridescent globes." '

'Precisely. I do not suggest that there is the explanation for these events. But if it is not then we are forced once again to accept coincidence in lieu of explanation. The description, such as it is, of the Great Old Ones, is selected from a period of less than thirty years in our own time. Let me illustrate finally on the subject of strange disappearances, taking no account of motivated disappearances, aeroplane vanishings, or similar cases.

'Dorothy Arnold, for instance. She vanished on December twelfth, 1910 somewhere between Fifth Avenue and the Seventy-Ninth Street entrance to Central Park. Absolutely without motivation. She was never seen again, no request for ransom, no survivor to gain, nothing.

'Similarly, the *Cornhill Magazine* records the disappearance of one Benjamin Bathurst, British Government representative at the Court of Emperor Francis in Vienna; with his valet and secretary, he stopped to examine horses he was to use in Perleberg, Germany. He walked around to the other side of the horses and simply vanished. Nothing thereafter learned of Bathurst. Between the years of 1907 and 1913, three thousand, two hundred and sixty of the people who had disappeared mysteriously in the city of London alone were never traced. A young man employed in a milling office in Battle Creek, Michigan, set out to walk from the office into the mill. He vanished. The Chicago *Tribune* of January fifth, 1900, records the case of this young man, Sherman Church. Nothing was subsequently seen of him.

'Ambrose Bierce—and here we come to something sinister. Bierce hinted of Carcosa and Hali—he vanished in Mexico. It was said that he was shot while fighting against Villa, but at the time of his disappearance he was virtually an invalid and was over seventy. Nothing further heard of Bierce. That was in 1913. In 1920, Leonard Wadham, walking in South London had a frightening lapse of normal perception, and suddenly found himself on a road near Dunstable, thirty miles away, without any knowledge of how he had got there.

'But let us come home, let us come to Arkham, Massachusetts in September, 1915. Professor Laban Shrewsbury, of 93 Curwen Street, while walking in a country lane west of Arkham, utterly and completely disappeared. Some evidence of expectation, for the Shrewsbury papers disclosed instructions that the house was to be unmolested for a period of at least thirty years. No motivation, no trace. But it is significant that Professor Shrewsbury was the only man in New England who knew more of these matters now before us, as well as of allied matters both terrestrial and astronomical, than I. So much for that. These instanced phenomena exist in proportion to the known and recorded similar phenomena as a ratio of an infinitesimal fraction to a million.'

After a long enough time to allow for the assimilating of this rapidly narrated series of curious facts, I asked, 'Conceding that the data in these rare books does offer the solution of the events which have taken place in this corner of the State during the past two hundred years and more, what then, in your opinion, is it—which particular manifestation, that is—that lurks at the threshold, which is presumably the opening in the roof of that stone tower?'

'I don't know.'

'But you suspect, surely?'

'Oh, yes. I suggest that you take another look at that quaint document, *Of Evill Sorceries done in New England of Daemons in no Humane Shape.* The reference goes back to "one Richard Billington" who "sett up in the woods a great Ring of Stones inside which he say'd Prayers to the Divell . . . and sung certain Rites of Magick abominable by Scripture." This is presumably the circle of stones around the tower in Billington's Wood. Now, the document suggests that Richard Billington feared and was finally "eat up by" a "Thing" he called out of the sky at night; but nothing in the nature of evidence is offered. The Indian wise man, Misquamacus, "charm'd the Daemon" to a pit in what had at one time been the centre of Billington's circle of stones, and had there imprison'd it under—the word is illegible, but it is probably "slab" or "stone" or something similar, "carved with what they call'd the *Elder Sign*." They called it *Ossadagowah,* and explained that it was the "child of Sadogowah," which suggests instantly one of the lesser known entities of the myth-pattern we have been examining: *Tsathoggua,* sometimes known as *Zhothagguah* or *Sodagui,* which is described as non-anthropomorphic, black, and somewhat plastic, Protean in origin, of primal worship. But the description ventured by Misquamacus differs from the commonly accepted one; he described it as "sometimes small and solid, like a great Toad the Bigness of many Ground-Hogs, but sometimes big and cloudy, with no Shape, though with a Face which had Serpents grown from it." This description of the face might fit Cthulhu, but the manifestations of Cthulhu are more closely associated with watery places, and most particularly the sea or places with ingress to the sea of greater proportions than the Miskatonic's tributaries offer. It might also fit certain manifestations of Nyarlathotep, and in this we are closer to home. Misquamacus plainly made an error in his identification, and he was in error also as to the fate of Richard Billington—because there is evidence to show that Richard Billington went out through that opening to the Outside, across and beyond the threshold to which Alijah makes such pointed reference in his abjurations to his heirs. The evidence is in your own ancestor's book, and Alijah was aware of it, for Richard came back in altered shape, and had some kind of commerce with humanity. Moreover, so much was known as legend to the Dunwich people, who may be presumed all to be in some fashion aware of the mythology and rites practised by Richard Billington, who initiated and instructed their ancestors. In Bates' manuscript, he reproduces Mrs. Bishop's oblique comment about the "Master." But to Mrs. Bishop the "Master" was not Alijah Billington; that is apparent through every document available and also in Bates' own manuscript even before he talked to Mrs. Bishop. This is what she says: "Alijah shut It up—an' he shut up the Master, too, out there, Outside, when the Master was ready tew come back agin after thet long a time. Ain't many as knows it, but Misquamacus fer one. Master walked the earth an' none knew him as Saw him fer he was in many faces. Aye! He wore a Whately face an' he wore a Doten face an' he wore a Giles face an' he wore a Corey face, an' he sat among the Whatelys an' the Dotens an' the Gileses an' the Coreys, an' 'twas none who knew him fer aught but Whately or Doten or Giles or Corey, an' he ate among 'em an' he bedded among 'em an' he walked an' talked among 'em, but so great he was in his Outsideness thet those he took weakened an' died, not being able to contain him. Only Alijah outsmarted Master—aye, outsmarted him more'n a hundred years after Master was dead." Does that suggest anything to you?'

'No, it is utterly incomprehensible.'

'Very well. It ought not to be, but we are all bound to some degree by thought-patterns based on what is logical and rational according to our store of recognized knowledge. Richard Billington went out through the opening he had made, but he came back through another—probably one of those experiments similar to Jonathan Bishop's. He took possession of various people; that is, he entered into them, but he was already a mutation from his existence Outside, and as least one result of his existence here in this secondary form was recorded in your ancestor's book, when he tells about what Goodwife Doten brought forth near Candlemas of 1787, a creature described as "neither Beast nor Man but like to monstrous Bat with human face. It made no sound but look'd at all and sundry with baleful eyes. There were those who swore that it bore a frightful resemblance to the Face of one long dead, one Richard Bellingham or Bollinghan"—for which, of course, read Richard Billington—"who is affirm'd to have vanished utterly after consort with Daemons in the country of New Dunnich." So much for that. Presumably, then, Richard Billington in either physical or psychic form, continued to exist in the Dunwich country, doubtless accounting for his share of the horrors which have been spawned there—the ghastly mutations which have so readily been dismissed as evidence of physical "decay" and "degeneracy"—for over a century, until, in short, the house in Billington's Wood was once more occupied by a member of that family. Thereupon the force that was Richard Billington, the "Master" of Mrs. Bishop's narrative and of the Dunwich lore and legends, once again became active in an attempt to restore the primary opening. Very possibly through suggestion from the outsideness which was Richard Billington, Alijah began to study the old records, the documents and books; eventually he restored the circle of stones, some of which he may have used in the construction of the tower—thus accounting for the greater age of some of the tower—and, naturally, he removed the block of grey stone carven with the Elder Sign, taking it from the vicinity, precisely as Dewart and the Indian companion he has discovered persuades Bates to remove it again on this occasion. Thereupon, the reopening was accomplished, and there began a curious and doubtless a memorable conflict—if only record of it remained. For Richard Billington, finding his end accomplished, set about to accomplish his secondary purpose, which was to resume his interrupted existence on this earth in his own house and in the person of Alijah. But, unfortunately for him, Alijah did not stop with accomplishing Richard's primary purpose; he continued to study; he obtained more of the *Necronomicon* than Richard had thought possible to find; he went ahead quite on his own and summoned certain of the Things from Outside, and permitted those Things to ravage the Dunwich country for whatever purpose they conceived necessary, and in this fashion he continued until he became embroiled with Phillips and Druven on the one hand, and on the other became fully and finally aware of Richard Billington's intentions, whereupon he sent the Thing or Things, and in all likelihood, Billington's force, back into the Outside, and simply sealed up the new opening with the stone bearing the Elder Sign, following which he took his departure, and left behind only a set of inexplicable instructions. But something of Richard Billington lingered, something of the Master remained—enough to enable him to accomplish his purpose again another century later.'

'Then the influence at work out there is Richard Billington, not Alijah?'

'Beyond question. We have certain indications of it. Richard is the Billington who disappeared and not Alijah, who died in his bed in England. It is therefore conflict which Bates mistakenly thought to be evidence of split-personality, and, only Richard could have inflicted himself upon the weaker Dewart. Finally, there is one little manifestation which is absolutely damning. Richard Billington has had enough traffic with those Outside to be subject to the same strictures to which they in their own dimensions are subject. In short, to the Elder Sign. Now, then, on the day on which the Indian appeared before dawn, you will remember that Dewart required Bates' help. It was to move away and bury the stone marked with the Elder Sign. Dewart "dared" Bates to lift it alone. Bates did so. Mark that, neither Dewart nor the Indian raised a finger to help— in short, neither touched it because he dared not—because, Phillips, *Ambrose Dewart is no longer Ambrose Dewart, he is Richard Billington, and the Indian, Quamis, is that same Indian who in Alijah's time assisted Alijah, and who more than a century before, in his own time, served Richard—summoned back from those terrible, blasphemous spaces Outside to begin again the horror begun over two hundred years ago!* And, if I mistake not the signs, we shall need to act swiftly and urgently in order to prevent and thwart that purpose, and no doubt, Stephen Bates will have further things to tell us when he pauses on his way home three days hence—if indeed he is permitted to come!'

My employer's foreboding was realized in considerably less than three days.

There was no public statement or announcement of Stephen Bates' disappearance, but there came to hand by way of a rural mail carrier, a torn fragment of paper which, he said, he had picked up on the Aylesbury Pike, and which, since it appeared to be addressed to Dr. Lapham, he had brought along and turned over to my employer. Dr. Lapham read the paper in silence and passed it over to me.

It was scrawled, apparently in fearful haste, and had the appearance of having been written while held against his knee and, later, the trunk of a tree, for the pencil had gone through the paper in various places.

Dr. Lapham. Misk. U.-Bates. He sent IT after me. Got away first time. Know It will find me. First the suns and stars. Then the smell—oh, God! the smell— like something burning long time. Ran when saw un- natural lights. Got to road. Hear It after me, like wind in trees. Then the smell. And the sun exploded and the Thing came out IN PIECES THAT JOINED TO- GETHER! God! I can't. . . .

There was nothing more.

'We are too late to save Bates, clearly,' said Dr. Lapham. 'And I hope we shall not meet what got him,' he added ominously, 'because against that we have poor power indeed. Our only chance will be to get Billington and the Indian while the Thing is back Out- side, for It will not come unless summoned.'

He opened a drawer in his desk as he spoke, and took from it two leather bracelets or arm bands, ap- pearing at first to be wristwatches, but proving to be leather bands holding an ovoid grey stone, on which had been carven a curious design—a rough star of five points, centered with a broken lozenge framing what appeared to be a pillar of flame. He handed one of them to me, and put the other on his own wrist.

'What now?' I asked.

'We're going out to that house and ask for Bates. It may be dangerous.'

He waited for me to protest, but I said nothing. I followed his example and put on the bracelet he had handed me, and then opened the door for him.

There was no sign of life at the Billington house; several of the windows were shuttered, and, despite a certain coolness in the air, no smoke rose from its chimney. We left the car in the drive before the front door, walked up the flagstones to the door, and rapped. There was no answer. We rapped again, more loudly, and again, until finally and without forewarning, the door was opened and we were confronted by a man of medium height, with a hawk nose and red hair in a flare about his head. His skin was dark, almost brown, his eyes keen and suspicious. My employer immediately introduced himself.

'We are looking for Mr. Stephen Bates, and understand that he stays here.'

'Sorry. He did. He set out for Boston the other day. That is where he usually lives.'

'Can you give me his address?'

'Seventeen Randle Place.'

'Thank you, sir,' said Dr. Lapham, and put out his hand.

Somewhat surprised at this unnecessary courtesy. Dewart reached out to take it; but his fingers had no sooner touched my employer's, then he gave a hoarse cry and leaped backward, clinging to the door with one hand. The transformation which came over his face was terrible to see; his previous suspicion changed to ineffable hatred and baffled rage—and, more—there was in his eyes an enlightenment. Only for one moment did he stand so; then the door was flung shut with shaking violence. In some fashion, he had become aware of the strange bracelet my employer wore.

Dr. Lapham, with undisturbed calm, led the way back to the car. When I slipped behind the wheel, he was gazing at his watch.

'Late afternoon. We have not much time. I expect him to go to the tower tonight.'

'That was in the nature of a warning you gave him. Why? Surely it would have been better not to let him know.'

'There is no reason why he should not know. It is better that he does. But let us not waste time talking. We have much to do before nightfall, for we will want to be out here before sunset. And we must get into Arkham for some things we will need tonight.'

Half an hour before sundown, we were making our way on foot through Billington's Wood, approaching from its western extremity, well out of sight of the house. A kind of twilight already held the thickly overgrown woodland, further impeding our progress, for we were heavily laden. Dr. Lapham had forgotten nothing. We carried shovels, lanterns, cement, a large jug of water, a heavy crow-bar, and various other similar paraphernalia. In addition, Dr. Lapham had armed himself with a curiously old-fashioned side-arm which shot bullets of silver, and carried the sketch Bates had left with us to show just where he had buried the large block of grey stone marked with the Elder Sign.

To avoid any needless conversation in the Wood, Dr. Lapham had explained that he expected Dewart—which is to say, Billington—and perhaps the Indian, Quamis, to come to the tower as soon as night had fallen and carry on their hellish practices. Our course up to that point was prepared in advance. Without delay, the stone slab must be recovered and made ready for use; cement must be mixed likewise and got ready. What happened afterwards depended upon Dr. Lapham, who had instructed me rigidly to make no interference and to be prepared to obey his commands without question. This I had promised to do, though with a fearful sense of foreboding.

We arrived finally in the vicinity of the tower, and Dr. Lapham quickly discovered the place where Bates had buried the stone bearing the seal. He dug it out easily while I mixed cement, and not long after sundown, we were ready to begin our vigil of watching and waiting while the dusk gave way to night, and from the direction of the marsh beyond the tower to the east came the demoniac pulsing and throbbing of the batrachian voices, while over the marsh a constant wild flickering and lightning betrayed the presence of myriads of fireflies, whose white and pale green lights made a constant shimmering as of an aurora in that place, and in the woods around us, the whippoorwills began to sing with a strange, unearthly cadence, and seemingly all in unison.

'*They* are nearby,' whispered my employer ominously.

The voices of birds and frogs rose to a frightful intensity, beating a mad cacophony into the night, pulsing in rhythm until I thought I could no longer tolerate that weird, infernal din. Then, when the chorus of voices had risen to its absolute wildest, there was a reassuring touch on my arm, and I knew without the necessity of hearing Dr. Lapham's voice, that Ambrose Dewart and Quamis were approaching.

Of the events of the remainder of that night I can hardly bring myself to write objectively, though they are now long in the past, and the countryside around Arkham has enjoyed a sense of peace and freedom unknown for more than two centuries. Those events began with the actual appearance of Dewart, or rather, Billington in Dewart's guise, in the opening of the tower roof. Dr. Lapham had selected the place of our concealment well; from it we could see through the foliage the entire frame of the opening in the tower roof, and in this leaf-framed opening, the shape of Ambrose Dewart presently appeared, and almost instantly his voice, raised in something uncouth and terrible, began to issue from his lips, calling out primal words and sounds with his head raised up to the stars, and eyes and words directed to outer space. The words came clearly, even above the madness of the frogs and the whippoorwills—

'*Iä! Iä! N'ghaa, n'n'ghai-ghai! Iä! Iä! N'ghai, n-yah, n-yah, shoggog, phthaghn! Iä! Iä! N'ghai, y-nyah, y-nyah! N'ghaa, n'n'ghai, waf'l pthaghn—Yog-Sothoth! Yog-Sothoth! . . .*'

A wind began to rise among the trees, a *descending* wind, and the air grew chill, while the voices of the frogs and the whippoorwills, and the flickering of the fireflies increased in tempo. I turned in alarm to Dr. Lapham and was just in time to see him take deliberate aim with his side-arm, and fire!

I swivelled my head around. Dewart received the bullet; he was knocked slightly back, but struck the frame, and pitched out headfirst to the ground. At the same instant, the Indian, Quamis, appeared in the opening, and in a furious voice continued the rite begun by Billington.

'Iä! Iä Yog-Sothoth! Ossadogowah! . . .'

Dr. Lapham's second bullet struck the Indian, who did not fall, but simply seemed to collapsed together.

'Now, then,' said my employer in a cold, grim voice, 'get that block of stone back in place!'

I seized the stone, and he followed with the cement, amidst the demoniac and terrible pulsing of frogs and whippoorwills all around us, and we ran, unmindful of underbrush, to the tower, for the wind grew in intensity, and the air chilled more rapidly. But before us loomed the tower, and in the tower the opening framed the stars—and, horror of horrors, *something more*!

How we got through that unforgettable night with the memory of that horror in mind's eye I do not know. I have only a vague recollection of the sealing of that opening—of the burial of Ambrose Dewart's mortal remains, now at last free in death of that malign possession by Richard Billington's evil presence—of Dr. Lapham's reassurance that Dewart's disappearance would be ascribed to the same unknown and undiscoverable source as the others, but that those who waited for his body to turn up as did the others would wait in vain—of the fine, age-old dust which Dr. Lapham said was all that remained of Quamis, who had been dead 'more than two centuries' and walked only at Richard Billington's evil command—of the tearing apart of that circle of stones—of the destruction and burial of the tower itself, *from below,* so that the dread grey stone with the Elder Sign on it would not be disturbed in its passage into the earth—of the discovery in that earth by lanternlight of curious bones many decades old, going back to that ancient 'Wonder-Worker . . . the Wampanaug head man Misquamacus' —of the complete breaking away of that magnificent study window—of the abstraction of valuable books and documents to be deposited in the Library of Miskatonic University—of the gathering up of our paraphernalia—of driving the car around for the books and documents from the Billington House—of our flight just before dawn. Of all this, I say, I have but the vaguest memory; I know only that it was done, for I forced myself to visit that one-time island in the tributary *Misquamacus,* so named in Richard Billington's time and given being by him in Ambrose Dewart's possessed tongue, and saw nothing, no sign remained of the tower and the circle of stones, the place of Dagon, of Ossadogowah, and of that other, that frightful Thing from Outside that lurked at the threshold waiting to be summoned.

Of all this, only the slightest memory, because of what I saw framed in that opening where I had expected to see but stars, and the charnel, nauseating smell that poured in from *Outside*—not stars, but *suns,* the suns seen by Stephen Bates, in his last moments— *great globes of light massing towards the opening, and not alone these, but the breaking apart of the nearest globes, and the protoplasmic flesh that flowed blackly outward to join together and form that eldritch, hideous horror from outer space, that spawn of the blankness of primal time, that tentacled amorphous monster which was the lurker at the threshold, whose mask was as a congeries of iridescent globes, the noxious Yog-Sothoth, who froths as primal slime in nuclear chaos forever beyond the nethermost outposts of space and time!*

SUPERB S-F
from
⒝⒝ BALLANTINE BOOKS

POLICE YOUR PLANET
 Lester del Rey and Erik van Lhin $1.50

A CASE OF CONSCIENCE James Blish $1.50

GATHER, DARKNESS! Fritz Leiber $1.50

THE BEST OF FREDERIK POHL
 With an INTRODUCTION by
 Lester del Rey $1.95

A GIFT FROM EARTH Larry Niven $1.50

MARUNE: ALASTOR 933 Jack Vance $1.50

THE BEST SCIENCE FICTION OF
 THE YEAR #4 Terry Carr, Editor $1.50

CLOSE TO CRITICAL Hal Clement $1.50

▼ Available at your local bookstore or mail the coupon below ▼

MORE S-F
from
ⓑ BALLANTINE BOOKS